Claws of Life

A TEDDYCATS NOVEL

MIKE STOREY

RAZORBILL

An Imprint of Penguin Random House

An Imprint of Penguin Random House
Penguin.com

ISBN 9781101998854

Printed in the United States of America

1 3 5 7 9 10 8 6 4 2

Book design by Corina Lupp

For all my grandparents

Chapter 1

BILL GARRA HELD the line as the glowing, green eyes of the shapeless intruders crept closer, gathering into sinister clusters. The Teddycats were locked together, prepared to defend Horizon Cove, their newfound sanctuary. They had endured a violent ouster from Cloud Kingdom and a long, deadly slog through the jungle—they had no choice now but to fight.

Those who were with Bill—Luke, Omar, Maia, and Elena; his mother, Marisol; other friends and family; even the Elders—were tucked behind him, while Diego, the fierce and loyal Teddycat scout, stood by his side in a defensive stance, wielding his hefty walking stick.

Bill snarled and dug into the soft grass of Horizon Cove. His teeth and claws were bared. There was no telling how many creatures they would face. It had never been Bill's intention to fight anybody, from the humans to the crocs to whatever threat faced them now. But responsibility for the well-being of his loved ones landed squarely on Bill's young shoulders, and he had led the Teddycats to this place, promising safety and security. He couldn't allow anything to rip that promise away.

Slowly, the narrowed eyes drew closer, accompanied by a hissing sound. Bill's heart beat with a bruising force, and his muscles twitched in anticipation. He would have to rely on ancient jungle instincts to protect himself and the others, but surprisingly, he felt prepared. He had matured a great deal since leaving Cloud Kingdom. His shoulders were wider, his muscles fuller. The challenges of the journey through the jungle to Horizon Cove—clashing with humans, saying goodbye to good friends—had given Bill a renewed focus on what, and who, was truly important. While the old Bill might have panicked right about now, the new Bill felt no urge to flee. Deep down, he knew what his father would do. With any luck, someday he would tell Big Bill about the showdown over the future of Horizon Cove.

"Get ready!" Bill yelled. His eyes were hot and stinging with adrenaline. Everything was fuzzy in the pale darkness, clouding the corners of his vision. All around him the other Teddycats tensed their muscles and held their breath.

Diego leaned in. "What do you see, mate?"

"Whatever they are," said Bill, "there are a lot of them."

"More of us," said Diego, though Bill couldn't figure how the scout was so confident of that.

"We'll see," said Bill. He turned around. "Mom, you and Maia and Elena get the Elders and hide in the trees. I'll come for you all when it's safe. Luke and Omar, stay close to Diego and follow my lead."

"We're not going anywhere," said Marisol, resting a warm paw on her son's head.

"There's nowhere left to go," said Maia, pulling her sister closer.

The intruders inched into focus: crocodiles, long and studded with scales, their tails whipping back and forth. The Cove was a part of their hunting territory, and they welcomed the Teddycats' arrival with open jaws.

Bill's fur stood on end. He had faced the crocs before, but never on this scale.

"Well, here we go," said Diego, in a rousing, gravelly voice. "Long live the Teddycats!"

The crocs were nearly within striking distance when a loud squawking descended on the Cove. Bill and Diego looked up as a flock of bulky birds flooded the moonlit sky. The squawks rose to a piercing shriek as the birds swooped down on the crocs, shielding the Teddycats with their wide wingspans and sharp beaks.

"What are these things?" Marisol cried.

The crocs seemed similarly flustered, angrily thrashing their tails and gnashing their teeth as the birds hopped up onto their heads and pecked at their eyes. The noise was almost unbearable as the birds' shrieking collided with the Teddycats' cries of panic, and Bill struggled to hold a plan in his head. The Teddycats had to take advantage of the birds' timely arrival and make a run for it! If they could make it to the tree line that beckoned from the back of the Cove, they could use their claws to climb to safety. But just as Bill turned to share his plan with the others, one of the birds scooped him up, lifting off the ground with a violent flutter of feathers.

"Hey, put me down!" Bill hollered.

The bird lifted further, dangling Bill from its claws. Bill jerked and flailed until he realized how high the bird had flown, and he watched as other Teddycats began getting plucked up by the birds. The biggest birds could carry three Teddycats at a time.

Bill could also see the crocs below him, clearly on the run and hustling back to the water, yelping in pain.

He spotted Maia and Elena in the clutches of one bird, his mother in another. The fear in their eyes was unmistakable. Bill was afraid too, but he realized that the birds—whatever they were—had saved the Teddycats from the crocodiles.

They flew higher, well above the trees. Had it been day, the view would have been striking. Bill wasn't scared of heights—after all, the Teddycats had once made their home in the clouds. But he had never been this high before. Dangling from a strange bird's talons was different from swinging from vine to vine. His hind legs kicked in the air as the talons dug into his chest.

The trees were far below, poking out of the darkness. He glanced up to get a better look at the bird, a sense of its intentions. But all he could see was the underside of the large, crooked beak. Below him, the rest of the Teddycats bellowed into the dark jungle as the birds carried them away from one danger but toward the terrifying unknown.

Chapter

2

AS THE BIRDS began their descent, Bill struggled to get his bearings. He could tell that they were in a densely forested corner of Horizon Cove, though it seemed to be a more protected area. The bird carrying Bill zigzagged through tangles of vines, interlocked tree limbs, and branches heavy with buds and fruit, finally landing in a clearing and releasing Bill. Bill scampered out of reach of the bird's talons, but his rescuer seemed suddenly uninterested in him. The rest of the birds landed, dropping Teddycats into the soft grass before stalking off into the brush.

Bill surveyed his surroundings. Moonlight drilled through an opening in the thick canopy and illuminated the clearing, which was shaggy and lush, ringed with large, well-built nests. They were roughly the same size as the Teddycat dens back in Cloud Kingdom. The birds' subtle, hidden habitat seemed at odds with their aggressive defense tactics and bright colors, but perhaps the one necessitated the other. For all Bill knew, the birds were on the run, same as the Teddycats. After all, this was the jungle—nature moved quickly, and life could change fast.

Bill hoped the two species, thrown together into a corner of Horizon Cove, would get along. The fact that the birds had saved them from the crocs was a good sign, but they could have been a bit friendlier about the whole thing. A simple introduction would have been a great start, an icebreaker on the way over.

Almost immediately, the other Teddycats mobbed Bill.

"What do these winged creatures mean to *do* to us?" asked Finn, a gray-bearded Elder, as the others wailed.

Bill wanted to tell them that he didn't know any more than they did, but he also wanted them to feel safe, to feel like they hadn't followed his lead for nothing. So as the Elders badgered him, demanding answers, Bill did his best to calm the Teddycats.

"Are we missing anybody? Was anyone left behind with the crocs?" he asked. The Teddycats murmured, counting heads. After a tense moment, Marisol came forward with the official count.

"We're all here," she said.

They might be shaken and unsteady, but the Teddy-cats were still together. The Elders sulked for a moment, but then turned their attention to Diego instead.

"What will we do now?" they asked.

"All right, easy now," Diego said. "Gettin' all worked up won't do any good."

With the Elders distracted, Bill managed to pull away from the mob and huddle with Marisol, Maia, Omar, and Luke.

"Anybody ever seen these birds before?"

"No way," said Omar.

"I tried to get a look at mine on the flight over," said Bill, "but the beak blocked me."

"Same here," said Maia. "When will they explain themselves?"

"Hopefully sooner rather than later," said Bill.

"If the Elders try to stick this on you, well, they can go climb a tree," said Marisol, her maternal instincts still on display.

"No," said Bill firmly. "We need to stay together, no matter what."

THE NIGHT DRAGGED on, with no word from the mysterious birds. The Teddycats huddled together as dawn crept through the canopy and the jungle came to life, a symphony of flutters and hisses, the cracks and crashes of falling trees. Bill and Diego kept watch while the others slept fitfully.

The Teddycats were anxious to begin their day as well. Most had gorged themselves on flowers and grasses upon first landing at Horizon Cove, but there had yet to be a proper meal. And on top of their current confusion, they were tired and dirty from their journey, their fur matted with mud and dew.

Diego nudged Bill and pointed across the clearing. The birds were emerging from huge nests, stretching in the morning light. Their colors were striking, and their bodies were oddly shaped and awkwardly posed, as if their insides had been patched together from loose materials. The biggest one strutted toward the Teddycats, leading the flock. It was pink and ruffled, with long spindly legs and a graceful tube of a neck. Bill had a hard time believing that these creatures could survive in the jungle with their awkward stance and colorful plumage, much less fend off a coordinated croc attack. But obviously the newcomers had much to learn.

The bird motioned for the Teddycats to gather and beckoned Bill forward.

"Please, gather around, everybody," the bird said. "My name's Pablo. I'm a Pet, and this is our home. I'm going to show you around."

"Did he say 'pet'?" Luke whispered.

"Shh," said Bill. "Just let him talk."

"Let's save all questions for the end of the tour, shall we? You there," said Pablo, pointing at Bill, "you follow me. Everyone else, follow . . . what's your name?"

"I'm Bill Garra."

"Everyone else follow Bill."

PABLO TOOK OFF with surprising land speed, considering his strange stance. As tour guides went, he was friendly and informative, barreling through what seemed to be a set routine. Bill and the other Teddycats just tried to keep up.

"This is our little gully of peace and quiet," Pablo said. "It's not much, but we love it."

Up close, the Pets' nests were densely woven, and they clung to the trees like ornaments.

"A bit of history about Horizon Cove," continued Pablo. "This location is part of our annual migratory pattern. It accommodates our colors and our lifestyle, and we're very protective of it, as it coincides with a very vulnerable period of our migration. Therefore, we have strict rules about who can enter and who must leave. Now, you call yourselves Teddycats?"

"That's right," said Bill.

"Well, the Teddycats have been deemed 'potentially compatible' by the higher-ups. The crocs, however, are not invited. And you saw what happened to them."

Pablo swatted his wings together gleefully.

"Thanks for that, by the way," Bill said. "It was a very impressive rescue. I don't know how much longer we could have held them off."

"If you don't really give 'em the business, they start to get ideas," Pablo said. "And before you know it you're inside a croc's belly, and that's not really part of *my* migratory pattern, if you know what I mean."

"We've had our fair share of run-ins with them before," Bill said, thinking of Maia and Elena's close call on the journey to Horizon Cove, the fevered snapping of the croc's jaws, his teeth gnashing as Elena dangled just out of reach. "But never anything on that scale."

"Where are you all coming from?" Pablo asked.

Bill exchanged glances with Marisol and Diego. Cloud Kingdom had once been a closely guarded secret, though these days secrecy didn't seem to matter. Diego offered Bill an approving crunch of the snout.

"We used to live in a place called Cloud Kingdom," Bill said.

"Sounds dreamy," said Pablo. "What brought you all the way down here?"

"Intruders. Humans."

"Ouch," said Pablo. "Humans are bad news. We don't allow them here. We are a strictly nonhuman enclave, and we employ guards and scouts, both in the air and on the ground. Once you get tangled up with humans, it's difficult to escape."

"We didn't *allow* them in Cloud Kingdom, either," Marisol said testily. "But that didn't much matter."

"You're right," said Pablo. "I'm sorry. What I meant to say was, we try to partner up only with those who share our diet, our values, and our lifestyle. So no humans, no big predators, nothing that will disrupt or destroy our beautiful but admittedly fragile ecosystem."

"And you think the Teddycats might be compatible?" Bill asked.

"All signs point to yes!"

"Have you ever 'tangled' with Joe?" Diego asked.

"What's Joe?"

"An especially nasty human," said Bill.

"Sounds like trouble," said Pablo. "I'll do my best to steer clear. But please, let's *try* to save questions until the end of the tour."

"Right," said Bill, "sorry."

"It's just a little thing," said Pablo. "I mean, hopefully it's interesting to you. For example, over here is our water source."

Pablo pulled back a curtain of palm fronds, revealing a beautiful trickle of clear water. It slipped down an ancient, lava-smooth gutter, collecting in a small pool. The others gasped with glee and instinctively began to surge forward. Bill thrust out his arms, trying to hold them back so they wouldn't immediately dive right in.

"It's fine," said Pablo, laughing. "Help yourselves."

Bill dropped his defenses, and the Teddycats rushed to the water's edge. They lapped at it with their tongues and scooped puddles with their paws. Bill was slightly embarrassed by their neediness, though he was thirsty as well.

As the Teddycats splashed and gulped, Bill took in his surroundings. He scanned the nests and the thick foliage, searching for signs of life. The Pets were obviously well established in this corner of Horizon Cove. Bill recognized much of the same infrastructure that the Teddycats had been so proud of in Cloud Kingdom—tended gardens, permanent dwellings, an orderly system of governance—but while the isolation and the eerie quiet suggested safety from humans, crocs, and other predators, there was also a spooky sense of having been snared. Bill couldn't exactly put his paw on why he felt so unsettled, though he figured this was how Cloud Kingdom would have felt to an outsider: welcoming, but vigilant.

Luke returned to Bill's side, dripping wet. "So, what do you guys eat?"

Pablo shook his head, then gave up. It was clear that the Teddycats were too curious to continue sitting on their questions. In their minds, they had already waited long enough. They wanted to get back to the way things were before the crocs advanced and the Pets descended. Those few hours alone in Horizon Cove had been the most peace they'd known in far too long.

"Straight to the point," said Pablo. "I like it. So as I said, this is part of our annual migration. We fuel up here for the long trip ahead, and once the rains come, we're out of here and you Teddycats can have the place to yourselves. You should be quite comfortable. There's plenty to eat, plenty to drink. The crocs shouldn't bother you all the way up here. So long as you stay away from the hunting grounds and keep to the Nest, you'll be fine."

"That's it?" Bill asked. "You'll just hand it over?"

"We're hoping you'll serve as stewards," said Pablo. "Protecting our home until we return next year."

Bill and Luke couldn't contain themselves. Each grinned widely at the good news. Bill hadn't let the Teddycats down or led them to doom—Horizon Cove would be theirs once again.

Diego noticed Bill and Luke's jovial mood, but he still had questions. "And when do you expect these rains?" he asked Pablo.

"Wow, you don't miss a thing, do you?"

"Not much, mate," said Diego.

"He's a great listener," Bill said.

"That's important!" Pablo said.

"On top of that," said Bill, "Diego is one of our fiercest, most trustworthy scouts."

"Pleasure to meet you," said Pablo. "So: Once the rains arrive, the Nest becomes a bit more treacherous, at least for us. With your claws I'm sure you'll have no problems. But the rain removes our primary foodstuff.

The worms rise to the surface just before the season begins, and then after the first storm the water washes them away."

"Worms are good eating," said Diego, smacking his lips.

"We had some good grubs in Cloud Kingdom," said Bill, "but we mostly ate sweetmoss."

"Ooh la la," said Pablo. "Sweetmoss? That's a little rich for our blood."

"I saw some earlier," said Luke.

"Yeah," said Bill. "We were just rollin' in it!"

"That was in the hunting grounds," said Pablo, exasperated. "This is why I asked you to hold your questions! Of course there's sweetmoss down in the hunting grounds, but good luck getting it without becoming croc food."

Just then, Omar, Maia, and Elena returned from the pond.

"I drank too much," said Omar, holding his belly.

"I'm starving," said Elena.

"That's not true," said Maia.

"Yes it is," said Elena, "I'm really starving."

"No," said Maia. "You're just hungry. There's a difference."

Bill knelt down until he was the same height as little Elena. "Pablo says they have plenty of worms to eat here. Does that sound good?"

Elena nodded excitedly.

"Don't get her too fired up," warned Maia. "At least until we actually see the food."

"Oh, we've got worms, all right," said Pablo. "Big ones."

Pablo wasn't kidding. The Teddycats watched as he dug into the ground with his sharp beak and then, with a few rough tugs of his neck, dragged out a worm as long as a root and as thick as a plantain. It writhed on the grass.

"Bill, would you do the honors?" Pablo asked.

Bill looked around. The Teddycats' mouths were watering. Even the Elders seemed transfixed. So he bared his claw and diced the worm into manageable slices. It cut easily, and the meat was clear and juicy. As he continued down the worm's length, Diego and Marisol began to distribute the pieces. Some of the Teddycats were whimpering at the sight. Finally, once everybody was happily chewing, Bill helped himself to a mouthful. It was very good.

"TOO BAD THE worms take off during the rainy season," Bill said during the digestive lull. "Guess we'll just have to enjoy them while we can."

"It's the circle of jungle life," said Pablo. "Can't try to change these things, you know?"

"Sure do," said Bill. "My old friend Felix taught me that."

"He was one of your Elders?"

"No," said Bill. "Well, sort of. He was a big, old cat. A jaguar."

Pablo seemed impressed. "He come with you guys?"

"He died on the way," said Bill. For a moment, he allowed his snout to lapse into a frown, and his eyes felt suddenly heavy. Felix's absence didn't always feel real, and Bill missed his courage and resolve. They would need all the help they could get.

"I'm sorry to hear that," said Pablo.

The sun was shining brightly, and rays cascaded through the canopy, so Bill shook off the chill of grief and continued on.

"You said the rains are coming," said Diego. "How do you know when they will arrive?"

"There are three signs," said Pablo. "First, a great, violent wind. We expect that any day now."

"How violent are we talkin'?" Diego asked.

Bill was grateful to have Diego around to take charge, since he was still distracted thinking about Felix.

"You'll recognize it," said Pablo, chuckling. "Trust me."

"And then what?"

"Then the water levels rise," said Pablo. "We think the rains come to the mountains first, and the water flows down here. That's what makes the worms come to the surface."

"You can't collect the worms before they're washed away? Save them someplace?"

"We've tried that before," said Pablo. "They don't keep all that well. Besides, we have to travel light. It's a long trip."

"So what's the final sign?" Diego asked.

Pablo straightened up. He was tall and imposing when he extended his neck. Bill noticed other Pets joining them as well. The nests around them shook as birds exited through their cramped hatches. Seeing them all together, it was hard for Bill not to think back to their attack on the crocs. The Pets were powerful, and there was a confidence about them that Bill had long felt the Teddycats lacked. If the Teddycats wanted to live in the jungle, to really carve out a place for themselves, they would need that same confidence and power.

The Pets converged behind Pablo, and the circle of tall grass seemed to shrink. Bill and the Teddycats were roused from their post-worm haze.

"The last sign is a fire in the sky," said Pablo. "Great crashes and booms. The fire can seem miles away and then split the tree right in front of you. I've seen it land on the river and burn up everything it touches. It's best for us to leave before that happens."

"It can't be all that bad," said Bill. "We had pretty rockin' storms up in Cloud Kingdom."

"Don't underestimate the rainy season," said Pablo. "It can be extremely dangerous. But as I've said, we think you're well suited to survive it and make the Nest a safer, stronger haven. So, what do you say?"

Bill turned to face the Teddycats. They huddled together.

"This could be home for us," Bill said. "It has everything we need: water, shelter, food, and companionship. We partnered with the Olingos before, so why not join with the Pets? To survive in the wild, we need to have friends. I think we should accept the Pets' offer of friendship. But I am not the only voice here. I know there are concerns. Let's hear 'em."

At first there was nothing but silence. A breeze in the trees and a rattle in the distance. The Teddycats seemed intimidated by the looming presence of the Pets. They didn't want to be rude.

Bill turned back to Pablo. "Just give us a second."

"Take your time," said Pablo. Some of the Pets behind him fluttered their wings impatiently, but most remained quietly imposing.

Bill and the Teddycats drifted back toward the pond. Though he was surrounded by family and friends—Teddycats young and old whom he loved and respected—Bill couldn't help but feel the absence of his father. And looking at his mother, he knew that she did too. Big Bill would know what to do. He'd have the answers, the words the Elders needed to hear to assuage their fears. But Bill didn't have those words on hand, not yet, and he needed those who were unsure to make themselves known.

"It's no Cloud Kingdom, that's for sure," said Finn.

A small chorus of grumbles joined him.

"You're right," said Bill. "It's not Cloud Kingdom."

"I don't see why we don't just race up these trees right here and start building a new Kingdom," said Armando, another Elder.

Bill had been hoping the journey to Horizon Cove had blunted Armando's pronounced defiant streak and general crankiness. Unfortunately, it might have actually made them worse. Armando was less civic-minded than Finn. In the end, Finn just wanted everyone to like him, and he would eventually work his way to a fair solution. But Armando cared only for himself. While this made him unpopular, he said what many Teddycats would think but dare not share, their worst impulses and beliefs. If given the chance, he would bully the others into submission, and the community would splinter.

"If we keep trying to go it alone we will never be safe," said Bill. He had been hoping Armando would refrain from chiming in. "We have to accept the dangers of the jungle and work with other species to try to make it better."

"Those birds are funny looking," said Elena.

A few other Teddycats laughed, and Bill looked to Maia for help. She smiled encouragingly, but it was clear she had no plan of her own.

"They *are* sorta funny looking," she said, pulling her sister closer. "But the humans thought *we* were funny looking, too."

"Exactly!" Bill said. "The Pets are surviving and thriving, even though their nature presents great odds and obstacles. Shouldn't we learn from them? Maybe our next home—"

"Our *next* home?" Finn yelled. "If you're going to take us on another wild *pollo* chase, then why bother teaming up with these whackos now?"

"This place is a rat hole," said Armando. "Let's go back to Cloud Kingdom. If I'm going to die, I'd like to die in my own den."

"That's not what you said when the humans were rampaging through the place," said Marisol. "You cried out to anybody who would listen, 'Save me, save me!'"

"How dare you mock my panicked cries!" Armando said. "I was in shock!"

"Nobody is mocking you," said Bill in a calming tone. "But if you go back, you won't find what you're looking for."

The Elders murmured, then receded to the rear of the crowd. The rest of the Teddycats seemed largely convinced, eyeballing the ample food and drink stockpiled by the Pets.

Diego sidled up to Bill. "Ask 'em how long they're stickin' around, mate."

"That's my only question," said Maia.

"Isn't that a little . . . pushy?" Bill asked.

"It's just plain sensible," said Diego, as Marisol nodded in agreement.

"I mean, they should absolutely take their time," said Maia.

"Of course!" said Omar.

"But it would still be nice to know . . ." Maia added.

Bill ambled back to Pablo and the Pets.

"Hey, Pablo," Bill said, hemming a bit. "When would you say—you know, best guess—but approximately when would you say you're expecting that wind to pick up and push you guys along?"

"Oh, any day," said Pablo, craning his neck to the sky. It was bright and still, the jungle air heavy as the sun slowly singed the mist. "Won't be long now."

"Right," said Bill.

"But look, we're happy to show you around, make sure you're comfortable, get everybody situated. It's in everybody's best interest for you guys to be in the best position possible to protect the home we've spent so much time and energy building."

"Well, I really appreciate that," said Bill. "Some of us are just a little . . ."

"They're in shock," said Pablo. He stretched his considerable wings, gesturing to all that the Pets were offering. "I get it. But the jungle doesn't always hold your paw as you figure out the next move. I would call this . . . a rare opportunity."

Bill nodded. He was deeply satisfied, almost walloped with gratitude for these strange birds who had saved the remainder of his persecuted species from near-certain death and very possible extinction. To Bill, the Elders' stubborn resistance wasn't just impractical, it was rude. If you asked him, the Teddycats should have been throwing themselves at the Pets' spindly feet, happily willing to do whatever was needed to make up this debt to their saviors.

But the Elders had always been the types to ask what you had done for them lately. A lifetime of service to their chosen causes would be discarded the second someone questioned their wisdom or decrees. It was almost shocking that they had survived this long. It was only thanks to the seemingly invisible Cloud Kingdom that the Elders had stayed safe, and now here they were, turning down perfectly good shelter because they didn't want to share or because it was beneath their ridiculous standards.

Bill took a deep breath. Pablo was right: The Teddycats were in shock. It wasn't their fault they were uneasy. Well, not completely. Some critters have to be dragged kicking and screaming into the future—or even the present. Bill had been spoiled by his old, enlightened jaguar pal Felix, a wizened jungle soul who had never resisted change and always embraced the unpredictability of jungle life. Good old Felix, who gave his life for the Teddycats. Now *that* was the kind of selflessness and sacrifice they needed.

Bill began to turn back to face the Teddycats but stopped himself. They had heard enough. There was no need for more negotiations. With the Elders unlikely to budge, Bill saw little reason to test the Pets' patience and generosity by trying once again to convince the ancient holdouts.

"We'd love to take you up on your offer," said Bill. He extended a paw.

"Hey, bring it on in," said Pablo, wrapping his wings around Bill in a warm, stifling embrace. Behind them, Teddycats cheered and scoffed. Deep within the folds of Pablo's plumage, Bill's snout twitched. The feathers were soft and contained a muffled heat and almost briny scent.

Just then, a screech splintered the sky.

Bill wiggled free of Pablo and staggered, scanning the canopy for clues. Every last hair on his body was rigid with panic. The rest of the Teddycats were similarly affected by the sound. It had been like a rip in the world, something that had escaped from another, horrible, deadly dimension. The Teddycats huddled in fear, their claws bared and at the ready.

Chapter

3

IT TOOK A while for Bill and the rest of the Teddycats to realize that the Pets were laughing. More than laughing, actually. They were doubled over, contorted, huffing and hacking on their mirth, their long necks shaking as they convulsed.

"Oh boy," said Pablo. "I guess you didn't have raptors up in Cloud Kingdom."

"What *was* that?" Bill asked, still shivering.

"Just a jungle hawk," said Pablo. He sized them up. "I wouldn't worry about them too much. You Teddycats are a bit big—they go for slightly smaller critters."

"But that sound!" cried Finn the Elder. "That shriek will haunt my dreams for the rest of my life."

Pablo brushed aside Finn's cries. "Hold on, where are my manners? You all must be starving again." The pinched faces of the Teddycats instantly relaxed. "How about some grub? Let's get you all fed and settled."

The promise of food calmed the Teddycats, and Bill was reminded all over again just how sheltered they truly were. They needed to adapt to life in the jungle, and fast.

THE TEDDYCATS' MEAL consisted of shredded carrion and pawfuls of fresh grubs and grass. Even though the Teddycats were traditionally herbivores, they had the good sense not to turn down a free meal. Pablo led them to the food reserves, and then Bill and the others congregated around a fallen, hollow tree trunk to chow down and rest.

"Not exactly my favorite," said Omar, digging in, "but I'll take it."

"Ditto," said Luke. "I've got a pretty tender belly."

"Olingos eat everything," said Diego. "They're scavengers, bottom-feeders."

"All right, take it easy," Bill pleaded. The last thing they needed was more fighting. "Get used to trying new things—we'll have to adapt if we're going to survive here."

"It's not half-bad, if you ask me," said Maia, her paws smudged with larval ooze.

Elena popped up, eyes wide. "I like the food!"

"That's the spirit," said Bill.

"Your father made me eat a lemur leg once," said Marisol. "It just tasted hard and bland to me, like unripe fruit, but not too bad."

"Out in the wild, you eat whatever you can to survive," growled Diego, picking his teeth with a freshly stripped bone. "Once, on an expedition, I slipped down a ravine and had to eat bats until my sprain healed enough for me to crawl out."

The others grimaced as the old scout spat at the memory.

"I think most of us are doing our best," said Marisol in a measured tone.

It was clear that she wished to leave room for Bill to thrive and lead. But he didn't want her to hold back too much—his mother was an experienced nurse and a brave soul, not to mention his main remaining connection to Big Bill.

As Bill chewed (and chewed, and chewed) his long-dead mystery meat, he noticed a young Pet frolicking on the outskirts of the clearing. The Pet was tugging on a dangling vine, trying to snap fruit off the tree. Several older Pets had already ordered him to stop, but the kid kept tugging until a cluster of nuts rained down on the flock. They scattered angrily as Bill laughed.

From under the tree, Pablo caught Bill's eye and walked over to where the Teddycats were eating. "How's it going over here?" he asked.

"Going great," said Bill, relieved that Pablo hadn't approached while the grumpy, whining Teddycats first inspected their new diet.

Bill pointed to the young Pet, still pulling on the vine. "Hey, Pablo, who's that?"

"That's Frank," said Pablo, rolling his eyes. "He's harmless, just a little whippersnapper."

"I don't know anyone like that," said Marisol, nudging Maia.

The two laughed.

"What?" Bill asked.

"Oh, nothing," said Marisol.

"You really don't see the resemblance?" Maia asked, smiling.

"What do you mean?" Bill said again, but his cover cracked and he broke into a bashful grin. Maia knew him too well. He did see a lot of himself in the misbehaving Pet. Back in Cloud Kingdom, Bill had barely been able to sit still long enough to be reprimanded for his most recent transgression. He felt pulled in multiple directions all the time, like he might explode if he stopped moving. Of course, that was before his epic journey through the jungle, before he had tasted true fatigue, hardship, and danger. He liked to think he was a bit more mature now, able to savor the good times rather than simply race to the future. A part of that had been because of his friendship with Felix, learning the cold fact that life could end at any time. Sometimes it still didn't feel real, like Felix might emerge from the brush and reassure Bill with his warm eyes and graceful, menacing prowl. If the jungle could take down Felix, it would have no trouble with anybody else, and the best Bill could hope for was time to spend with his family and friends and a better chance for future Teddycats to do the same.

Still, the little Pet was fun to watch. Bill's paws itched a bit. His hind leg began to shake. It had been a while since he'd really let go—not counting the total panic of the croc attack—and it would do him good to climb a tree sometime soon. But Bill ignored the tug of the wild. The future of the Teddycats was in his paws—they had to become established jungle citizens before the winds picked up and blew the Pets away.

Chapter

ONCE THE TEDDYCATS had feasted, Pablo led a tour of the nests. They were remarkably similar to the Teddycats' dens in Cloud Kingdom—large and homey, with cool, damp corners—but of course the Elders still found plenty to complain about. As usual, the grumblings were led by Finn and Armando, who muttered under their breath from the back of the procession.

"If only our ancestors could see us now," said Finn. "Squatting in piles of sticks, eating filthy bugs."

"This is no place for a Teddycat," Armando snarled.

"Hush up," Bill growled, rushing back to confront the Elders. "Right now. If you turn the Pets against us, we have nowhere else to go."

"And whose fault is that?" smirked Finn.

"Don't doom us all because you want to see me fail," warned Bill. His claw itched, but pulling it on another Teddycat would be a serious offense.

Still, the other Teddycats seemed cowed, and cleared out of Bill's way as he returned to Pablo's side. He was embarrassed, but grateful to Pablo for choosing to ignore the old-timers' complaints.

"Wow," said Marisol. "*Hush up*? You almost sounded like me back there."

"Just trying to keep us moving in the right direction," said Bill.

"Here's the good news," Pablo continued, pecking at a nest's frayed weave of vine and bark. Bill noticed his feathers bore a strange tint, though it could have just been a trick of the jungle light. "The nests are all yours, as soon as we head out for the rainy season. Just pick whichever one you'd like and move on in."

Bill peeked inside a nest, where a Pet tended to her sleeping young. Bill noticed the same sour smell from Pablo's feathers, but he didn't want to complain. *The Pets' signature fragrance will wash away once they migrate,* he thought to himself. And the rains would help; they would give everything a good, strong scrub.

THE ELDERS CONTINUED their grumbling. "I don't see any sweetmoss," said Armando, contempt dripping in his voice.

Beyond their petty complaints, Bill could see the fear in the eyes of the Teddycats as they timidly skulked about the clearing, following Pablo.

Thrust into a new habitat, the Teddycats were out of sync with the jungle. Cloud Kingdom had allowed them to live in peaceful seclusion, with everything exactly as they liked it. This made it difficult for the Teddycats—especially the Elders—to imagine any other way of life. They would need to learn to live in true harmony with the forest, learn to accept its savage whirlwind. Otherwise, they were doomed.

Sweetmoss was the least of their concerns, but Bill only patted Armando on the back.

"Don't worry," said Bill. "We'll find something for your sweet tooth."

PABLO'S TOUR CONTINUED as he poked through the nests at a leisurely pace. Though the other Pets were friendly and welcoming, they were mostly quiet. *Probably tired from the croc battle,* Bill thought. Each nest featured something like a birdbath in its center: a column made from mud and dried grass that held a deep scoop of water. Even the Teddycats, for all their engineering ingenuity, didn't have indoor plumbing.

"What do you think?" Bill asked as the Teddycats watched a Pet arise from slumber and crane its neck until its long, puckered beak reached the basin and took a deep, smacking drink. "I could sure get used to that."

"It's a li'l ripe in here," mumbled Diego.

"What was that?" asked Pablo.

"He said, 'Everything you need is right here!'" Bill answered quickly, stepping between Diego and Pablo. Bill felt like he was juggling jackfruit while simultaneously rolling a log down the river. And the last time he rode down a river he dropped off a waterfall and almost went under for good. "I think we're just really excited about getting in here and making it our own."

"Of course," said Pablo with a smile and a nod.

The tour ended in the garden, where the Pets maintained a loose arrangement of nutritious plant life and rotten logs that attracted slugs and grubs. The Pets had a more diverse diet than the Teddycats, but their cornerstones were recognizable: a blend of sweet grasses and soil-rich larval proteins, plus whatever remains they were able to find. While valued as found treasure by most jungle dwellers, carrion was considered garbage by the Teddycats. But Bill had to admit that the lunch he had just wolfed down left him feeling flushed and energized, almost angry. He figured that was the blood making its way through his system. Either that or he really needed to find a tall tree to climb.

Luke sidled up to Bill with a suspicious slant to his snout. "Bill," he whispered, "see those wet willows over there?"

Bill followed Luke's glare to a juicy bunch of wet willows sprawling at the foot of a rubber tree. They looked robust, with thick stalks and heavy tendrils.

"How is it they can have wet willows if they aren't around to plant them during the rainy season?" Luke whispered.

"Go ahead and ask Pablo," urged Bill. "I bet he'll have an answer for you."

Pablo was mid-ramble, something about seedlings. The garden, though crooked and disorganized, was stuffed with tasty edibles and nutritious treats. A set of boulders was covered with a delicious moss, dark, rich, and crawling with long, hairy bugs. The foot of nearly every tree was dotted with varieties of mushrooms and other delectable fungi. While Bill had just enjoyed a heavy lunch, his stomach was already growling in appreciation. He peeled a pawful of the dark moss from a rock and offered it to Armando, who scowled as he chewed.

"Excuse me," said Luke. "Mr. Pablo?"

"How can I help, little man?"

"Just a question," said Luke.

"A *quick* question," said Bill.

"Sure thing," said Pablo. "Shoot. And please, it's just Pablo."

Luke puffed up his chest and cleared his throat. "How do you grow wet willows if you leave Horizon Cove before the rain?"

"Good eye," said Pablo. "Those particular wet willows we plucked from the riverbed and replanted here."

"Smart thinking," said Bill. "How come we never thought of that?"

"See," said Pablo, as he snapped a drooping frond into two pieces, "that's why they're so juicy."

The Teddycats licked their lips as beads of moisture formed along the frond's crack.

"And that's how they're able to survive the rains."

Bill stared at Luke. "See?" he mouthed.

Luke seemed unconvinced. "I still say a real wet willow would drown during the rainy season. Everything takes a serious beating."

"Pablo just gave you a totally reasonable explanation!" said Bill, now fully exasperated. He couldn't believe that even a good friend like Luke, who had risked his life during the Teddycats' mad trek through the outer reaches of the jungle, was finding fault with this new home. Was it too well-appointed? Too convenient? Too available? Bill just couldn't understand the negativity. Who cared *how* the wet willows got to Horizon Cove? They were there! Next thing Bill knew, the Teddycats would be turning down free figs and mud baths.

"You don't understand, Bill," Luke said. "You've never seen the rains up close. What you had in Cloud Kingdom—that was nothing compared to a real monsoon."

"Oh boy, here we go again," said Bill.

Bill was sensitive about his relatively sheltered upbringing, and Luke knew it. As an Olingo, Luke had a front-row seat to the carnage and chaos of the jungle, while the Teddycats, the Olingos' one-time neighbors and allies, had fled to the trees. Bill was proud of his friendship with Luke—he wanted it to be a model for Teddycat–Olingo relations in the future, proof that the two species were stronger together—but Bill knew that their experiences had been very different.

"I'm just saying," Luke continued, withdrawing slightly from Bill's side and into the crowd of Teddycats, "Mr. Pablo's explanation makes less sense if you've ever lived through the rainy season."

"I told you," said Pablo, the edges of his beak frozen in a determined smile, "it's just Pablo."

"Whatever you say," said Luke.

The air felt thick with tension. Bill decided that they had seen enough of the garden. It was time for the Teddycats to be helpful. They would show the Pets that they could contribute to the cause by doing what they did best: climbing trees.

"Hey, Mom and Maia," said Bill, "why don't you guys figure out the sleeping situation while Luke, Omar, Diego, and I help Pablo scrounge up some dinner for later?"

"Sure thing," said Marisol. "We'll get everybody settled.

"We're bunking up!" called Marisol. "It's gonna be tight at first, but we'll make it work."

"I appreciate it, Bill," said Pablo, "but we've got dinner all ready. Just say the word and I'll ring the bell."

"Ah, but do you have anything for dessert?" Bill asked.

"Bananas?" asked Luke, suddenly no longer sullen or preoccupied with the origins of every other little thing. "Cashews?"

"We'll see what we find," said Bill. "What do you say, Pablo?"

"Let's do it," said Pablo. "And I'll bring Frank."

Out of the corner of Bill's eye he saw the little Pet leap out of an odd contortion and rush toward Pablo. Meanwhile, the rest of the Teddycats dispersed. Some sought quiet shade, while others mobbed Marisol, putting in rooming requests and other suggestions for the cohabitation plan.

While Bill waited for the crew to come together, he sized up surrounding trees, scanning the canopy for fruits, nuts, and other treats. While it was true that the Pets could fly and therefore had some access to the jungle's bounty, their awkward shape made it difficult to navigate the dense canopy. The Teddycats could claw their way right to the top and strip a tree bare in mere minutes, then either rain down fruit or pass the pawfuls to a waiting accomplice.

Bill was excited to get up in some trees. He was itching to climb. Between the carrion lunch and the leftover adrenaline from the croc attack, his heart was thumping.

The jungle seemed to bend down and invite him up into its highest reaches.

Something tugged on Bill's arm. He turned. It was Maia.

"Got a sec?" she asked.

"Sure," said Bill. "What's up?"

"I'm happy to help your mom," said Maia, "but don't give your guy friends all the fun gigs, okay?"

"What do you mean?" asked Bill.

"I was the one who broke you out of the human camp," said Maia. "I snuck defenseless Teddycats out of Cloud Kingdom as it was under siege. I was the one who found Luke and Omar, and I was the one at your side when you led the way to Horizon Cove. I want you to lead, Bill. It's what you were meant to do. But don't leave me behind. I want to help the Teddycats, too. I want to build a home. For Elena, for all of us."

"I guess I didn't want to overwhelm you," said Bill. "Or something. But I'm sorry."

"And you know I could outclimb all those dolts," said Maia. "I love 'em, but still."

"I haven't forgotten everything you've done for me," said Bill. "For all of us. So what do you say, want to come forage with us?"

"I don't want your mom to get torn apart over there,"

said Maia. The Teddycats really were scrapping over their nest assignments.

"Back off and get in line!" yelled Marisol, using the same tone that had kept the Cloud Kingdom hospital humming.

"Thanks a million," said Bill. "And I promise, you're my go-to wingwoman, my varsity squad cocaptain, my copilot, and . . ."

"Okay, all right," said Maia, laughing. "Get out of here. And bring me back something sweet."

Chapter

5

THE CASHEW TREE was fifty feet tall. It was dwarfed by other evergreens, but its mass of wide-reaching limbs made it appear more formidable. The canopy was a thicket, unwelcoming to those—like the Pets—who would try to swoop up from under to reach the clusters of cashew fruits. Omar and Luke gathered the colorful toadstools that grew among the raised roots, slicing the stems with their claws. Pablo and Frank stood side by side as Bill explained his cashew strategy. Diego looked on, somewhat dismissively, as he continued to sharpen the bone he'd been carrying around since lunch. It now featured a gleaming, dart-sharp point.

There were some minor flutters amid the leaves as Bill pointed out his targets. Because the ground was soft and there weren't too many of the group hanging around the tree, it would be safe to allow the cashews to simply rain down. That was always a happy sight, food literally falling from the sky. Bill hoped the Pets would appreciate it as well. He was still smarting from Luke's wet-willow investigation and wanted to make sure Pablo and the others knew how grateful their guests were for the continued hospitality. Well, most of them.

"So your claws, are they for climbing?" Pablo asked.

"Climbing and meal prep, mostly," said Bill. "We aren't really supposed to use them all that much, except for self-defense, obviously."

"Obviously," said Pablo.

"That's enough about the claw," said Diego. "Don't go blabbin' all our secrets, mate."

"Hardly a secret!" said Pablo. "You all can't quit flashing the dang things."

Frank hooked his talons and made a silly face, miming a Teddycat ready to strike.

"Ha!" said Pablo. "That's a good one."

Frank continued to hop around with his "claw" out.

"I get it," said Bill.

Frank filled his cheeks with air, then began to hoot and scratch his belly. He was inching closer and closer to Bill as his impression morphed into some loose combination of jungle dwellers.

"All right," said Pablo, "now that's just a monkey. Give it up, Frank."

"Sorry, Uncle Pablo," said Frank, still giggling.

Bill looked up at the tree again. "We could shake enough cashews out of this tree to last us all through the rainy season," he said, unable to hide the excitement in his voice. He was determined to prove to everybody that he understood what the monsoons would bring. The Teddycats would prepare sufficiently enough to stay well fed throughout the swampy season. "There was never a shortage of food in Cloud Kingdom, even during the drought years."

"What do you know about the drought years?" growled Diego.

"My mom and dad told me all about it," said Bill. He was surprised by the scout's challenge. He counted Diego as a close confidant and reliable advisor. Bill figured he was still getting over Frank's comic portrayal, which seemed aimed more at knotty Elders like Diego, rather than younger Teddycats like Bill and Omar. And Big Bill had regaled his son with tales of the drought years, as well as other natural near disasters.

When Bill was just a kitten, his father would tell him a story every night, always something about the resiliency and determination of the Teddycats. But gradually Bill got older and grew tired of those stories. He wanted to hear about the rest of the jungle, everything that was off-limits. By the time Bill took his first tumble out of Cloud Kingdom and down through the canopy to the jungle floor, his father steered clear of his straw pile and kept his stories to himself. Even so, there were many that Bill still knew by heart, word for word. He also knew that the drought years were what had led his mother to become a nurse. The sight of others in pain brought out the best in her, and she dedicated her life to alleviating that suffering—at first just for Teddycats, but eventually she convinced the Elders to let other creatures recuperate in the Kingdom's nurturing environment. Remembering the strength and good deeds of his family gave Bill a little boost of confidence. They were leaders, and he was lucky to have had so many opportunities to learn from them.

"Stories about the drought ain't the same thing as watchin' your family suffer," said Diego. "But go on, get your nuts."

"Thanks," said Bill, cocking his head and flashing his teeth. "I will."

FRANK GRABBED TIGHTLY to the fur of Bill's back.

"Hold on!" said Bill.

"Woo hoo!" yelled Frank. "Show me what you've got!"

"Let's not get the little guy too riled up," said Pablo. "This whippersnapper's bedtime isn't too far away."

"We'll be back in a jiff," said Bill. "Just watch."

Frank's wings folded under Bill's arms as his feet dug into his back. The little guy was heavier than Bill had anticipated, and he wasn't completely free of that telltale Pet scent, though it was fainter and milder than Pablo's. Bill took a deep breath, squatted down, and launched himself onto the cashew tree's thick trunk.

The higher they climbed, the darker and more fragrant the canopy became. The bark was drab, the cashews clustered between deeply shaded limbs. It felt great to climb. Bill's eyes narrowed in concentration, his muscles doing all the work by memory. Ever since Bill was born he'd had a fascination with climbing, finding the highest point and surveying all he could. Of course, no matter how high he rose, the jungle always looked endless. In fact, Bill's first memory was the sight of Cloud Kingdom's tallest tree. Just a kitten at the time, he fell over backward while craning to see the top, staggering in the shade as his parents watched, laughing. But those days were long over. Now Bill had a hard time believing there was a tree out there that he couldn't climb, or that a view of the forest could still bowl him over the way that tree had when he was young.

THE WIND RAKED his fur as Frank whooped in his ear. Bill remembered carrying Luke all the way up to Cloud Kingdom on his back. He remembered the pride he felt when they vaulted over the Wall and the entirety of the Kingdom was suddenly visible. Luke's dumbfounded reaction had let Bill experience the sight for something like the first time, all over again, and for that he would always be grateful to his friend. The fact that Cloud Kingdom's demise was tied to that one seemingly harmless and innocent transgression was easier to swallow now that they had found a new home.

The clusters of cashews beckoned, and Frank helpfully pointed them out.

"There's a big one!" he yelled.

"Comin' right up!" Bill hollered, his voice catching the wind. His eyes watered as he and Frank climbed and scampered across the knotty, busy branches. If Frank hadn't been catching a ride on his back, Bill would have just wrapped himself around the limbs, knocking loose the clusters on both sides. But he wasn't sure how ready Frank was to be inverted, and he didn't want to risk dropping his charge right in front of Pablo.

One by one, the cashews began to fall. They hit the grass silently, though some landed on rocks and cracked open. Luke and Omar immediately quit what they were doing and began to cheer Bill on. Even Diego got into the spirit. Once the lower branches were shaken clean, Bill and Frank continued toward the canopy's upper reaches. There, the clusters were fewer and farther between, but the fruits glowed with a dewy coating.

"Let me try one," said Frank, and before Bill could even agree, the Pet was leaning over the side and waving his wing at the broad leaves that covered the hanging drupes.

"Take it easy," warned Bill, though he could tell by the talon digging into his hindquarters that Frank was in no real danger of falling loose.

They continued to climb, until the leaves began to thin and the clusters ceased. Finally, Bill reached the top and poked his head out of the canopy. The view was relatively contained—the Pets' sanctuary was surrounded by towering evergreens and sheer rock faces—but it was still a sight worth taking in. From this vantage point the Pets' home looked cozy and inviting, overflowing with abundance and activity. Bill could make out the Teddycats at work under his mother's direction, as some of the little kittens played in the grass. Pets looked on as the Teddycats helped themselves to food, water, and shelter. Everyone seemed to be getting along, and Bill was thrilled. Pablo was right—the Elders and other naysayers were just in shock and simply needed time to adjust.

"What do you think of the view?" Bill asked.

Frank scrambled up until he was practically standing on Bill's head.

"There sure are a lot of you," said Frank.

"Yep," said Bill. "And there could be even more on the way. What do you know about the Olingos, Frankie?"

"Olingos?" Frank shrugged. "I heard they're unreliable."

"Furthest thing from it!" Bill exclaimed. "Olingos are some of the bravest warriors I've had the honor of fighting alongside."

"Whatever," said Frank, losing interest and turning back to the tree. "Let's get nuts already!"

Bill was again struck by the unfairness of the Olingos' reputation. It seemed like the whole jungle looked down on them, and the worst part was, the Teddycats were to blame for these stereotypes and misconceptions. If they had stuck with the Olingos or allowed them up to Cloud Kingdom, they wouldn't have been forced into lives of hardscrabble scavenging. Bill was determined not to make the same mistake here in Horizon Cove. It was time for Luke to reach out to his family. It was time for the Olingos and the Teddycats to reunite.

The cashews continued to fall. Bill could just make out the sounds of Luke and Omar racing around and celebrating the size of the haul. Luke could have as many as he wanted—he would need the energy for his imminent journey back to the Olingo den.

Chapter

"**BUT I DON'T** want to go back there," whined Luke, slumped between two heaping piles of cashews. "I just got here."

"Believe me," said Bill, "I get it. Horizon Cove is just starting to come together—and we just got all these cashews—but think about how great it'll be to have your family with you as it does. Everyone together again! Isn't that what we all want? Wasn't that why we stuck together despite all the dangers?"

"I guess," mumbled Luke.

"Personally, I'd love to see Freddy and Doris. I want to see what they can do to this place."

"The Teddycats hate the Olingos," said Luke. "Maybe you don't, Bill, but lots still do. Including him!" Luke glared at Diego and jabbed a paw toward the old scout.

"Don't drag me into this, mate," said Diego. "I've got too much else on my mind."

Bill popped a cashew and chewed thoughtfully. "You're right, Luke. It's a complicated relationship, and we've got a lot of work to do."

"Complicated?" spat Luke. "I'm not sure that's how my family would describe it."

"But don't the Olingos deserve the peace and security the Pets have offered us here?" Bill asked. "I wouldn't say this if I didn't think it was the right time to act, Luke. I know you can make the journey. And this is what we always talked about, the Olingos and the Teddycats together again!"

"Well, maybe we could all go?" Luke asked. "For old times' sake?"

"Hey, you know me," said Bill. "I'm *always* rarin' to jump on an impromptu jungle trek. But I have to stay here, buddy. There's too much to be done. If I take off now, Finn and Armando will keep on complaining until they poison the group. And to be honest, I think your Horizon Cove message will be better received by the other Olingos without me there, muddying up the joint."

"I ain't goin' nowhere," said Diego. "I'm retired."

"And man, do you ever deserve it," said Bill. "The Pets will be out of here any day now, and after that, surviving here will be our sole responsibility. So Luke, you go get the Olingos, and Diego and I will make sure there's a nice Cove waiting for you all when you get back."

Luke still seemed unconvinced, and Bill couldn't blame him. There had to be some way to make Luke see that he had to be the one to lead the Olingos to Horizon Cove, the same way Bill had led the Teddycats. Bill understood the weight of this responsibility. It could feel heavy and at times, impossible. But the hardest part of the journey to Horizon Cove had been the sense of aimlessness. Luke had a set destination, and Bill believed that his friend could make it back.

And the Olingos would be crazy not to follow Luke. They had to respect his courage, after he'd escaped the humans so many times. For all their history with the Teddycats, surely the Olingos would recognize a lifeline when one of their own presented it.

"What if they want to stay in the old den?" Luke asked quietly. His ears were twitching, which they tended to do when he was extremely anxious. "What if they want me to stay with them?"

"You can always come back here," said Bill. "You'll always be welcome."

Ears twitching, lips bit, eyes cast downward, Luke chewed himself up trying to keep it together in the face of this decision. "And you really think this is the best thing to do?"

"I can't decide the future of the Olingos," said Bill. "Only the Olingos can do that."

"Ha," spat Diego.

"*But*"—Bill glared at Diego before turning his attention back to Luke—"I'll help in any way I can, and we'll be here at Horizon Cove, ready to welcome you back with open arms."

"And don't forget your cashews," said Diego.

"I'm suddenly not so hungry," said Luke.

"That's just pre-journey jitters!" said Bill. "Totally normal. A good sign—means you're serious, on the edge of adventure."

A part of Bill wanted to join Luke. To be there for Luke just like Luke had been there for him. Plus, it was always thrilling to venture into the heart of the jungle. There was no telling what one might encounter, and that was still deeply appealing to Bill, who always wanted to see something new. But the trouble with growing up—one trouble, anyway—was that, it turns out, not everybody wants the same thing. Suddenly Bill had an idea.

"You know what, Luke? I've changed my mind. I will go with you."

Luke's eyes split wide open, as did Diego's.

"But . . ." Luke stumbled to respond. "What about Horizon Cove?"

"Yeah, what of it, mate?" asked Diego.

"Eh, I'm sick of it," said Bill. "All these Teddycats depending on me. It's just too much. I mean, who really cares what happens to them?"

Luke's features grew pale. "Bill," he said, his voice filled with dismay, "you're talking about your family and friends! Your mom, Maia, Omar, Elena . . ."

"Yeah, well, they're not my problem anymore," said Bill. "What do you say? Let's scram, hit the jungle, raise some trouble."

"I don't know," said Luke. In the distance they could hear the patter of industrious Teddycats attempting to merge their lives with those of the Pets. It was obvious from the slant of his jaw that Luke was conflicted: He wanted Bill to accompany him, but he also wanted a bright future for both the Olingos and the Teddycats. "I think you'd better stay here."

"After all that?" cried Bill. "Come on!"

"If you leave, who'll be in charge?" Luke asked.

"I don't know," said Bill. "Diego?"

"Ha!" said Luke.

"I told ya, I'm retired," said Diego.

"Fine," said Bill. "I'll stay. But you'd better hurry back."

"I will!" said Luke. "Now gimme those cashews!"

ONCE LUKE LEFT, the jungle suddenly fell quiet. The silence was both menacing and nurturing. Bill felt a bit bad about sending his best friend off into the wild, but he knew that if Horizon Cove was going to thrive, they would all need to be pushed past their limits. The lingering bad blood between the Teddycats and the Olingos would never fully fall away until the two species were reunited. But it wouldn't be easy, especially as the Teddycats themselves were barely united in this line of thinking.

Diego limped over to Bill. His constant companion, that ragged walking stick, found its way between the blades of Bill's shoulders, the sharp corners scratching away the same way his mother's claw once did. A shiver shot down his spine, and for a moment he felt tears gathering in the corners of this eyes. Whether this was due to Luke's farewell, his father's continued absence, or the general unrest ever since the croc battle, he didn't know, but the tears were tempting. Instead, Bill cleared his throat and batted away the stick good-naturedly.

But Diego saw through the performance. "You did the right thing."

"I didn't want to trick him into leaving," said Bill.

"It's for the best," said Diego. "He'll be fine."

"You really think so?"

"I give the li'l guy a hard time," Diego said with a snort, "but he's tough as they come. Back on our journey there were plenty of opportunities for him to turn tail and take off, but every time he stuck with us. That's the sort of thing I don't forget."

"That's true," said Bill.

Overhead a trio of Pets flew toward the Nest, their wings brushing the canopy as they descended, their feathers so flooded with light they seemed nearly aflame, though the patches of bare skin between the plumage were a sickly, transparent white.

Bill turned to face Diego. "I know Luke wasn't

totally convinced about Horizon Cove and the Pets, and I can accept some hesitation from the Elders, but I gotta ask, what are your reservations?"

Diego stretched as he thought. His body broadcast the many adventures its owner had seen throughout the years: scraps and brawls with other species, the everyday tangle of the jungle, the cuts and bruises of a million scouting jaunts and gathering expeditions. These scars were his reward for a lifetime spent defending a home, a community.

Seeing them, Bill felt young and foolish, tiny and unprepared. Obviously someone like Diego should be in charge, an experienced and trusted leader, someone capable of guiding the Teddycats into the Horizon Cove era by reminding them of their proud past. What had Bill ever done for his species, besides cause trouble? He glanced at Diego's scars once more, then turned away as his tears returned.

Finally, Diego stroked the gray bush at the base of his jaw, and his eyes softened as he spoke. "I think it'll be just fine, once we air the place out a bit."

Bill laughed. "It *is* a bit funky, isn't it?"

"Mate, when I first stuck my head in one of them nests I thought I might lose my lunch. But hey, I've dealt with much worse in my day."

"I know you have," said Bill. "You've seen—and smelled—so much. When I think about all you've done I just don't see how I can be in charge. The Elders will never listen to me. They'll turn the Pets against us, and then we'll be right back where we started from."

"If not worse," said Diego.

They sat for a moment. Bill popped a cashew. It was delicious, sweet, and chewy. He hoped Pablo and Frank were stuffing themselves full of them, telling every other Pet about the bounty Bill had brought raining down.

"Here's the deal, kid," said Diego. "I followed you out in the wild, and I'll follow you here."

"I know, and I appreciate it," said Bill. "But I just don't understand *why*."

"The jungle's a mystery," said Diego. "One thing I know: You don't really *choose* a leader. Everybody just follows their guts. So you follow yours, and I'll follow mine. Somehow, it'll all line up."

"You're sure about that?"

"Hey, you led us here," said Diego, idly scratching a scar. "And many thanks for that. But this is the jungle, mate: The chaos never ends."

Bill thought back to the challenges he'd already faced, the way the jungle always seemed prepared to deal some final, devastating blow, and how despite those dangers, animals kept going on with their lives, raising their families, playing with their friends, growing up, and growing old.

"I still feel bad about tricking Luke," said Bill.

"Yeah, well, these foul birds and their shifty colors are makin' me dizzy," said Diego. "We've all got our burdens to bear."

Chapter

IT SHOULDN'T HAVE surprised Bill that his mother had managed to make Horizon Cove sparkle in just the short time he had been gone, but nevertheless he couldn't help but pull a double take as he returned to the clearing. Dusk light filtered down through the trees, dappling the moss-coated stones, the rippling pool, and bunches of orchid blossoms.

Best of all, the cleanup effort seemed to have drawn the Pets and Teddycats together, as a pleasant, predinner din surrounded the garden.

Marisol was curled up outside her newly claimed nest. It was one of the more modest structures, so close to the jungle floor its base brushed the tall grass.

"I figured you'd choose one of those," said Bill, gesturing toward the larger, more protected havens high in the trees.

"Well, I thought it was time for a change," said Marisol. "If we're going to live in the jungle, let's really mix it up."

"Thanks, Mom," said Bill, nuzzling Marisol's thick, soft fur.

They snuggled in together and watched as the gloaming draped their corner of the Cove in golden light. Bill felt happy and safe, almost like he was back in Cloud Kingdom. All that was missing was his father, but he didn't want to ruin the moment by dwelling on Big Bill's absence. That seemed like a shortcut to an unhappy existence.

"It is beautiful, isn't it?" Marisol said, sighing.

"Sure," said Bill, his eyes closed, snout burrowed in his mother's chest.

"Still, it's strange to be in Horizon Cove. It hasn't quite hit me yet. The Cove has always loomed so large in Teddycat lore, I feel like I've gone back in time." Marisol smiled at the thought. "Though I do wish your father could be here to see this, and to see you."

Bill popped his head up. "I was just thinking that."

Marisol nodded, then said carefully: "Do you think about your father a lot?"

"Of course," said Bill. "I mean, every now and then. But we've been so busy, I guess I'm mostly afraid that I'll forget him."

Marisol laughed so hard her belly rumbled and the vibrations reminded Bill of long afternoons spent in his mother's lap. "I don't know, kid. Your father is pretty unforgettable. And in my experience, no matter the foe or the odds, he's always right around the corner."

Ever since Bill was a little kitten he had admired his mother's unflagging optimism. It was an inspiration, and a powerful force for good. Marisol, through pure grit and good cheer, was able to convince the Elders that bringing numerous injured creatures to Cloud Kingdom was worth the risk, and her esteem had only grown in Bill's eyes since his own dealings with the Elders. When he was younger he thought of his parents as two separate entities: His father was the muscle, while his mother was the one with the soft touch. But now he saw them as a single unit, two vines twisted together into an unbreakable bond. It was an image that brought him comfort, as did the knowledge that Big Bill would always beat in Marisol's heart.

"Luke went back for the Olingos," said Bill.

"Oh, good luck, little Luke," said Marisol. "I'm sure

he'll be just fine, and if he can't convince them to leave, nothing will."

Bill perked up. "That's what I said!"

"This reunion has been a long time coming. The Olingos will make Horizon Cove a better place, and they'll make the Teddycats better citizens of the jungle. Working together, the Teddycats and the Olingos presided over a long period of peace in Horizon Cove, a peace that spread all the way across the jungle. If we can recapture even some of that spirit, all of this will have been well worth it."

"But still, I felt guilty," said Bill. "I sort of had to trick him into setting off. Well, maybe not 'trick,' but it felt a bit mean."

Marisol shook her head. "You're a motivator! And besides, we all have new roles we'll have to get used to."

Soon, Pets began to break away from the garden and return to their nests. With the Teddycats occupying a good number of them, many of the Pets had to move in together, and not all of them seemed excited about their new arrangements.

"Why don't you go run and play while I finish up dinner?"

"Are you sure?" Bill asked. There was much to be done around the Cove. Some Teddycats were still wandering the clearing aimlessly, frazzled and out of sorts. But he was restless—the cashew adventure notwithstanding—and there was plenty of exploring to do. He had almost no sense of Horizon Cove's perimeter, which they would need to patrol and secure once the Pets left.

"Let me handle this," said Marisol. "I wouldn't want you to go nuts over the small stuff. Everyone will be in a better mood after a big meal and a good rest."

"It's always worked for me," said Bill.

BILL SCURRIED THE short distance from his family's new den to the drinking pool. He took several deep laps, and while catching his breath, noticed his quivering reflection. He was surprised at the sight: He didn't feel any older or bigger, but the Teddycat in the water had a heft and purpose that Bill had always associated with adult Teddycats—Elders and scouts and others swelled with authority. His snout was bristly, his coat lustrous and nearly overgrown. The changes frightened Bill a bit, but he couldn't help but be excited too. He looked the part, and now he would have to work hard to see himself as others saw him.

After a few more gulps of the cold, clear water, Bill decided to follow the trickle that fed the pool, knowing that even the smallest stream would lead to something bigger. He pushed through the brush that ringed the clearing, then through the low swaying palms and flowering vines. At times the stream collapsed into muck and swamp, but soon enough it reappeared. Just as the current began to pick up and the channel began to widen, Bill ran smack into a tall, jagged series of cliffs. The water cascaded down in wide sheets as Bill crept backward, scanning the bluff for a clue. Bill narrowed his eyes. These rock faces were different than the ones that had shielded Cloud Kingdom from predators and other unwanted visitors. While Cloud Kingdom had been forged from lava over the span of thousands of years, these rocks had a different sort of character, as if they had been assembled—or even carved—by some powerful, menacing force, something with the strength and conviction to alter the very shape of the jungle. Bill shuddered.

These cliffs had the humans written all over them.

Chapter

8

A GIGGLY, HIGH-PITCHED chortle sliced through the sound of rushing water. Bill yanked his eyes up to the sky. On the ledge of the bluff sat a small, piggish creature, its snout dangling over the edge. Bill laughed—it was a tapir, one of the jungle's strangest inhabitants. While scarce around Cloud Kingdom, tapirs were something of a running joke, seemingly defenseless creatures that nonetheless wiggled their way to a sustainable place in the jungle hierarchy. The tapirs were the clowns, the mystics, a slightly otherworldly presence in a wilderness too often defined by its ruthlessness.

Bill had never spoken to a tapir before, but he had always been jealous of their trunks. Eating would be so much simpler if he could just suck the grub through a tube attached to his snout! No more digging, no more cleanup. Another reason to be jealous: The humans had no use for the tapirs, which left them much freer to maneuver about the jungle. Of course, there were other serious predators on their tails—the jungle was a whirlwind of shifting positions on the food chain—but at least their fortunes weren't completely tied to the evil whims of old Joe.

Bill wanted to get closer, and the tapir did seem to be beckoning to him. But the cliff did not ease off into a gentle, sloping hillock. To reach the top, he would have to start at the very bottom, where the angle was extremely unkind. It would be a challenge even for a brave, veteran, beclawed mountaineer like Bill Garra. The tapir giggled again, wagging its trunk. There was something between its teeth, something Bill couldn't quite make out, but it was clearly meant for him. Bill sighed, bared his claws, and raced toward the rocks.

THE CLIFF WAS dimpled and curved, slick with dew and every slimy little thing that grew in the watery shadows. Only a hundred feet into the climb Bill found himself dangling, his hind legs poking at nothing, an eerie wind brushing his fur. His muscles burned with fatigue, but there was always a way forward—crags and ledges, some even deep enough for him to crawl into and rest. The falling water was a constant roar, though by the time Bill was halfway up, it had simply merged into white noise. Somehow, though, he could still hear the lively grunting of the tapir, the characteristic snorts of its snubbed snout and semiclogged trunk.

Sparks flew as Bill's claws scraped, slashed, and dug at the stone. He came upon a cluster of colorful fungi, swiped a few, and popped them in his mouth for extra energy. As he chewed, he turned to admire the view. While it was smart not to look straight down while climbing (even the most well-seasoned Teddycat could be struck by vertigo), Bill always enjoyed taking in a scenic vista. From the vantage point provided by the cliff, Bill could see for miles: the golden pocket of Horizon Cove, silver slivers of bending rivers, thick blankets of valley fog, and the endless green drizzle of rolling jungle hills. Instinctively his eyes surveyed the expanse, searching for a glimpse of Cloud Kingdom, but of course that wasn't possible; it was permanently shrouded in dense coverage, squeezed between two volcanoes.

The mushrooms were delicious but gritty, their fleshy gills sticking to Bill's teeth and tongue. He spat out the rest in a wet clump and watched it fall for as long as he could, falling and falling until it shattered in the wind, breaking his own don't-look-down rule until a shiver of fear shot him back upright and launched him like a catapult. Soon the tapir came into focus on the edge of the bluff, its eyes wide and playful, its trunk wiggling between them.

As soon as Bill crested the ledge the tapir rolled over and began to play in the grass. Bill caught his breath as the tapir sunned his belly in the last remaining rays of light. His shoulders ached and tingled in the pleasurable way they always did after a hard climb, but his head was spinning after the dizzying ascent. He took deep gulps of the thin air until his vision cleared and he could finally see what the tapir had clenched in his teeth. It appeared to be a long, drooping feather.

"What do you have there, buddy?" asked Bill.

The tapir dropped the feather and nudged it in Bill's direction. There were teeth marks imprinted on the shaft, but the barb and the colorful plumage were bright and intact.

"I'm Bill, by the way."

The tapir snorted and smiled. It was black with white streaks, though its snout and trunk were a light purple. The thin fur was smooth, almost rubbery. Bill leaned forward in anticipation as it slowly opened its mouth, but still it formed no words.

A gust of wind blew through, nearly toppling Bill and stinging his eyes. At that elevation the wind was strong and brisk, its embedded moisture striking and lashing Bill's skin with the force of a hard rain. But the tapir, with its round belly and low center of gravity, stayed safely plopped in the bent grass.

"Bill . . . Garra?" said Bill. Still nothing but a puzzling, blank smile from the plump little tapir. "Teddycats? Cloud Kingdom? Come on, give me something. Did you see what I just climbed?"

Bill gestured toward the ledge, and the tapir struggled to its feet and began to waddle in that direction.

"Hey, whoa, careful there," said Bill, stepping between the creature and about a hundred-yard tumble. "That's a long way down, my friend."

The tapir nodded in Bill's direction. He glanced down and saw the feather. It was a bright pink, almost electric. While similar in size to a Pet's feather, it hardly seemed to match their color scheme.

"Where'd you find this?" Bill asked.

The tapir just giggled. It was beginning to get on Bill's nerves.

"I get it," said Bill. "You're shy. Don't worry about me, I'm just here to say hello. Thanks for the feather, I guess. Be careful out there. Maybe next time we'll meet on more even ground."

Another wet gust of wind whistled past them. The tapir wore a sweet smile. Bill softened up and tucked the feather behind his ear. He was set to apologize for his gruffness when the tapir cooed something.

"Wait—what was that?"

"Raffi," said the tapir. "My name, Raffi."

"Now *that's* what I'm talking about!" said Bill excitedly. "Great to meet you, Raffi. As I said earlier, I'm Bill Garra, and we've recently set up camp over at the Nest, in Horizon Cove."

Introductions aside, Bill expected a fresh volley of new information from Raffi, but there was only silence. Well, jungle silence, which wasn't really silence at all, but more a steady, lively racket, as the systems of life kept moving forward. From the monkeys in the trees to the frogs on the palms to the grubs in the soil, Bill's triumph over the rock face and stumbling conversation with Raffi were among millions of daily dramas occurring simultaneously throughout the wilderness. Still, he would've appreciated an answer. And just as Bill prepared to break the silence, a distinctive call shot through, familiar but long gone. It was Big Bill.

Chapter

"DAD?" CRIED BILL. He ran to the ledge and peered over. Down below, not much more than a speck, stood Big Bill Garra, a small crowd of Teddycats behind him.

"Are you up there, son?"

"I'm up here!" Bill hollered. "I'll come down as fast as I can."

"Be careful," said Big Bill.

"See ya around, Raffi," said Bill, his father's stern warning still echoing as he dropped over the ledge.

Big Bill was always an imposing force, but Bill had never seen his father so haggard and battle-weary. His fur was patchy and rough, marred and slick in the places where he had bled. One hind leg was hitched up, giving him an off-kilter tilt, and one eye was nearly swollen shut.

"Dad, are you okay?" cried Bill.

He wanted to embrace his father, grab him tightly and hold on, but he didn't want to hurt him. The last time Bill saw his father, they had been in a very different place, under different circumstances. Cloud Kingdom was under threat, there was dissension in the ranks of the Elders, and Elena was missing. And all of that—in one way or another, unfairly or not—could be tied to Bill. So a dark cloud had lingered over their last meeting. And while Big Bill's absence had enabled his son to come into his own as a leader, and while Bill had never doubted that his father was alive and coming to find them, there had been moments of uncertainty, weakness, and fear.

"I'm fine and dandy," said Big Bill. "Now come over here and give your old pop a hug."

Bill scooted into his father's open arms. At first he tried to be gentle, but old instincts took over and he pressed against his father's chest, pulled by a force that he had almost forgotten. Big Bill grasped him tightly around the shoulders and squeezed.

Once they finally separated, Bill's eyes were glazed. The relief and excitement had him almost unsteady. Slowly, the clump of Teddycats accompanying his father came into focus. They were Elders, and some of them—

like Finn and Griff and Armando—wore scowls, their pain over the loss of Cloud Kingdom blinding them to the possibilities of the jungle.

"Luckily, one of these guys saw you head up past the water," said Big Bill.

"Very convenient," said Bill with a tight smile. He didn't like the idea of the Elders keeping tabs on his whereabouts and activities, but he couldn't say it surprised him.

His father cleared his throat. "I have something to tell you, Bill: Cloud Kingdom has been completely destroyed. Ransacked beyond all repair. I wish I had better news to share, but after the humans captured as many Teddycats as they could, they set the place on fire."

Now the dourness of the Elders made more sense. Bill felt his own features go long, drooping with grief. His shoulders sagged and his bones felt too heavy to bear. For a moment he thought he might collapse. The idea of Cloud Kingdom extinguished from all existence ripped a hole straight through Bill's heart. Here was a place that had survived geysers of lava and mountains of tumbling boulders, every arrow and plague the earth could muster, and it withstood each test, adapting and enclosing but still boasting life and community. Until the arrival of the humans, there wasn't a single affront the Kingdom couldn't withstand. The thought of it burning simmered in Bill's mind—he felt a heat rising through him and flushing his face.

"How did you survive?" asked Bill.

"I was lucky," said Big Bill. "Many others were not. And there's more, son."

Bill closed his eyes and braced himself.

"Joe is tracking me," said Big Bill. "Right now, as we speak. We do have scouts on the lookout, relaying his location, but with Joe's superior advantages we have to assume that he will find us sooner rather than later. That means we need to get underground. We gotta button this place up, and quick."

"Joe is *still* after us?" cried Bill. "Will the humans ever leave us alone?"

"He won't stop until he has the claw of every Teddy-cat in the jungle," said Finn. "This is why I said we should've built a new home in the trees. That's *our* advantage. We can't possibly defeat Joe out here in the open!"

"Hold on now. You say the Pets are filthy and odd, but they must have some experience defending the Cove. I'd say that's an advantage we could use right now."

"I don't trust them!" Finn argued, his paws balled into fists.

"And what have they done to rouse your suspicions?" asked Big Bill.

"Nothing!" said Bill. "The Pets have been nothing but kind and generous. We owe them our lives. They saved us from the crocs, offered food, water, and shelter. The Elders just can't see beyond a few minor housekeeping details. We can't waste time—we have to warn the Pets that the humans are coming."

Bill was close to frantic. Horizon Cove could not meet the same fate as Cloud Kingdom. He refused to let everybody down again—and this time the Pets were in danger as well.

"Why are the Elders even here with you?" asked Bill. "If they really wanted to help, they should have stayed by the Nest. They just wanted to be here when I got the bad news. But I've faced off with the humans before. They can be beat, but we've got to be smart and act fast."

Big Bill was silent for a moment, brow furrowed as he considered their diminishing options. When he lifted his head, he met Bill's eyes directly.

"Lead the way, son."

Chapter 10

THE TEDDYCATS RUSHED down the creek, back toward the Nest. Bill was determined to warn the Pets of the impending danger before Joe reached them, but their progress was hampered by Big Bill's injuries, as well as the Elders' frailties and sluggish acceptance of the plan.

Visions of a wrecked and ravaged Cloud Kingdom rattled in Bill's mind, with the residents and geography of Horizon Cove bleeding into the edges with the force of a premonition. Finally, after nearly stumbling down a jagged knoll, Big Bill gave his son permission to break away from the pack and run ahead.

"No sense in waiting for us," said Big Bill, shrugging off Bill's assistance and the grumbles of the Elders. "By then it could be too late."

He didn't have to say it twice. Big Bill never did. The second Bill recognized the determination in his father's eyes, he bid a lightning-quick farewell and then sprang into action, darting through the swamp muck and skipping over stones when the water began to course once more. Gradually the tree limbs began to bend to the current, sprouting thick, dangling vines, and Bill picked up speed as he swung between them. His fur prickled as he gained momentum, and for a brief, dazzling moment he forgot the dire reason behind his mad dash and savored the rush. This was what he most missed about Cloud Kingdom, which had afforded him countless breakneck descents to the jungle floor, and it was still how the forest made the most sense to Bill, when his instincts took over and his mind calmed. The visions of destruction dimmed, then disappeared entirely. There was only what was right in front of him. As his old friend Felix the jaguar would say, "In the jungle, the only move that counts is your next one."

Back and forth, Bill swung across the river, his paws only occasionally brushing the surface. The trick was to keep his eyes forward and accept the energy of his surroundings. There was no way to fight the jungle. To survive, you had to fold into it, catch an invisible wave. Soon his father and the Elders were far behind, and Bill's destination began to come into focus.

Except the closer he came to the Nest, the less he recognized. As he slid into the drinking pool, the entire settlement seemed to have been absorbed into the surrounding wild. The brush was dark and forbidding, seemingly seething with lurking malice. Bill's blood chilled—had Joe already razed the whole place, reducing it to nothing? Suddenly an urgent whisper broke through the mysterious quiet.

"Over here!"

Bill spun around, searching for the source of the sound. It sounded like Pablo, but he couldn't be sure. "Pablo?" he croaked.

When that was met with silence, Bill almost cried out for his mother, before remembering the task before him. He scanned the space for signs of Joe, but there was no smoke, no acrid, greasy cloud. But there was no sign of the Pets or the Teddycats either.

Just when Bill was close to giving up, turning around, and setting back to find his father and the Elders, the Nest began to shake. Not just the trees and the brush, but the whole gully, lightly and then with increased fervor. As it shook, the structures began to reveal themselves. First in mere glimmers, but then the dense foliage split wide open, and there were the Pets and the Teddycats, safe and sound, enclosed and protected by comprehensive camouflage.

Bill's jaw was slack with shock. Cloud Kingdom had been just about the most well-protected little pocket of the jungle, but the Pets had developed something entirely new: the ability to hide in plain sight.

He tried to warn the Pets about Joe's progress, but when Bill opened his mouth nothing came out. The sight before him was still too otherworldly. The Pets were cackling with stifled laughter, while the Teddycats stayed burrowed in the folds of the forest.

Finally, Frank swooped out of the mysterious void, wings wide but flight pattern askew, and landed beside Bill in the freshly emerged clearing. There was the garden; there were the nests and the path toward the water; there were the rocks and the wildflowers. All was as it had been before Bill left.

"How did you *do* that?" gasped Bill.

Frank chuckled. "Oh boy, you shoulda seen your face!"

"I was totally lost."

"Yep, we can shut her down pretty good," said Frank. "It's easy once you get the hang of it. We got the trees to mesh, and the rest is just brush and junk all tasseled together."

"Wow," said Bill. "We didn't have anything like this back in Cloud Kingdom."

"You didn't need it," said Frank.

"Well, until you did," said Pablo, landing with an awkward thud. Despite everything, Bill continued to be amazed by the difference between the Pets' appearance and their abilities. Looking at them on the ground, one would never believe that they could fly.

"You're right about that," said Bill, "and now Joe's on his way here."

Pablo scoffed. "You wouldn't have found us in ten moons if we hadn't made noise. No predator can, and you want to know why?"

Bill didn't feel like following up, but it seemed the polite thing to do. "Why?"

"Because predators, basic predators, are fools. They bare their teeth or their claws and stomp about, but despite their power they never dig deeper, because they've never had to."

Bill had to agree that Pablo had a point—he'd seen Joe and crocs and other bad actors trample and gnaw through whatever stood in their way, but he'd never seen an apex predator peel back the layers of the wild. They did seem to favor what was right in front of them. Still, Pablo seemed dangerously confident in the Pets' ability to avoid detection. At one point in time the Elders had been just as cocky.

"I'm very impressed," said Bill, "but let's put everything back the way it was—Joe could be here any second!"

"All right," said Pablo. "Places, everybody."

The Nest began to shake once more. Bill watched the Teddycats squeeze in order to make room for the retreating Pets. He hurried toward them.

When Bill spotted his mother he realized he had been so baffled by the Pets' disappearing act, he'd forgotten all about his father's triumphant return. "Mom!" he cried. "I saw Big Bill!"

"Oh, Bill!" said Marisol, scampering down the latticework of roots and branches and into her son's arms. "Is he really okay?"

"Yes!" said Bill. "He found me! Well, the Elders spied on me and then led him to my location, but anyway, he's back!"

"We're a family again!" Marisol exclaimed, her eyes brimming with tears, and as she shuddered in relief, Bill finally realized the full weight of her worry. But now Big

Bill had rejoined the Garra clan, and they could really get to work on building a new home.

The Nest continued to rumble and shake as the Pets kept filing in.

"Wait a sec!" Bill shouted. "We gotta wait for my father! Hey, Pablo, wait for my dad!"

Pablo paused just long enough to acknowledge Bill's cries, but immediately resumed ushering the Pets into hiding.

Bill comforted his mother. "I'll go talk to them. There's no way we're leaving him out here all alone with Joe on the prowl."

"Go ahead," said Marisol, her cheeks still wet. "I'll wait here."

Bill shot back out to the clearing. Pablo was overwhelmed, directing traffic and prepping the place for another disappearing act.

"Hey, how long will this take?" asked Bill. He was slightly out of breath and he realized he hadn't stopped running or climbing since his conversation with the little tapir. He brushed a paw behind his ear; the feather was still there.

"Not long," said Pablo. "Though once everything's set up we usually stay tucked away for a while, hibernating until the danger passes. We don't usually open and close like this."

"That's fine," said Bill. "But we can't leave my father out in the open. He's heading down the creek with some of our Elders."

"Don't worry," said Pablo. "I'll keep an eye out for them."

"Thanks," said Bill. "Means a lot."

Bill returned to his mother's side. To his surprise, she was talking with Frank. They were both laughing.

"What's so funny?" Bill asked.

"Oh, nothing," said Marisol. "Frank's just being fresh."

Bill turned to Frank. "Thanks for showing me the ropes back there," said Bill. "I was . . . kind of freaking out. But I didn't know you guys already had such great defensive measures in place."

"You got it, bud!" said Frank, lightly punching Bill's shoulder.

Bill smiled. Despite Frank's oddball, immature manner, he knew a great deal more about life and survival in Horizon Cove than any of the Teddycats, and so Bill was thankful for his friendship.

"So what do we do now?" Bill asked.

"Hunker down!" said Frank. "That's my favorite—nothing to do but veg out!"

THE HIDING SPACE grew increasingly dark, hot, and crowded, until the patchwork of greenery unraveled once again and there stood Big Bill, his arms crossed in triumph. He no longer seemed hurt—in fact, he looked great, ringed by passive Elders and a halo of late-day jungle light. He wore a cocky grin that Bill had seen only on rare occasions. Bill and his mother hurried through the crowd of Teddycats and Pets to the clearing, embracing Big Bill for quite some time. When they finally pulled apart, Bill stepped back and saw that his father's injuries still remained, but his pain was overwhelmed by the joy of their reunion.

"You made it!" said Bill.

"I was right behind you the whole time," said Big Bill, rubbing his son's head.

"But the Nest, and Joe . . ."

"Our scouts say Joe has veered wildly off course. He's nowhere near Horizon Cove. I passed on the intel to Pablo on the ground here, and we decided it was safe to go about our daily business."

"Sounds great to me," said Marisol. The tears had returned to her eyes.

Bill didn't want to watch her cry anymore, even if they were tears of joy. He spun about wildly, searching for his friends. "Hey, Maia, Omar, Diego—check it out: My dad's back!"

Big Bill raised his paw, and all the Teddycats cheered.

Chapter 11

THE MORNING WAS bright and cool in the shade. The Garras had fallen asleep in a big pile on the floor of their new den. Bill woke first and decided to give his parents some peace. He slipped out of their nest, down to the clearing. Pets were already working in the garden and piling debris around the drinking water. Bill ambled toward the project, yawning a bit. He was happy to help, though a lot of other things and ideas were tugging at his time and attention. For starters, it felt like forever since he had spent any time with his Teddycat friends. Life in Cloud Kingdom had been pretty much one long daydream, a glorious idyll spent scrapping and playing,

collecting fruit and nuts, and he was ready to settle back into that pace and schedule. And he missed Luke more than he had expected. Bill vowed not to take his friend for granted once he returned with the Olingos. Luke deserved better, and he would get it.

Bill was also hassled by thoughts of Raffi. Whenever he spotted the cliff looming in the distance, he was reminded of his lingering suspicion that the mysterious creature had something to tell him. Something important.

Polly, a Pet with especially droopy eyes, was overseeing the work.

"Hope you're ready to put in a full day," said Polly.

"Good morning," said Bill. "What do we have here?"

It appeared that the Pets were reinforcing the creek banks to accommodate the coming rains. Bill had some experience with that line of work. In fact, he and Luke had once been the proud owners of a secret fort up by Cloud Kingdom, and they had been in the process of damming up a creek to create a swimming hole.

"What we *have here* is a high-priority project," said Polly, with the cadence of a jungle hornet, stinger out. "Playtime's over. Round up your 'Cats so we can assign gigs."

"Why don't you tell me a little bit more about—"

"The rains will be here any day," said Polly. "We're happy you're here, but my schedule doesn't have any more flex. So let's move."

Polly turned to the flock of Pets already carrying bits of bark and leaves. "You hear that? Let's move, everybody."

The Pets grumbled but picked up the pace of their awkward shuffling and waddling.

"Sounds great," said Bill carefully. "I'll go tell my parents. See you soon."

He slowly backed away, but Polly was no longer paying attention, so he broke into a run. His stomach was growling with hunger when he returned to the Garra nest, where Pablo was waiting.

"So, I see you've met Polly," said Pablo with a chuckle. "Sorry if she scared you. She can be a little intense."

"Just a little," said Bill. "Obviously we're all happy to help, and we appreciate everything the Pets have done for us . . ."

"Slow down," said Pablo. "We're just capturing the water so there's sure to be enough for you all once we're gone. The real surprise is this: We're buildin' tree houses, Bill! That's right, the Teddycats will return once more to the canopy. Welcome home!"

ONCE PABLO LEFT, Bill informed his parents of the Pets' plan. He didn't focus on Polly's attitude or Pablo's bluster—he just wanted everybody to share a common goal.

"If this is going to be our home, we should have some say on these projects," said Bill.

"Let me talk to this guy," said Big Bill, gathering steam.

"Maybe hold off for a moment," suggested Marisol, rubbing her husband's sore muscles. "You're still recovering from your journey."

As a nurse, Marisol had mastered the ability to soothingly suggest a course of least resistance. She had managed to treat boars and bobcats side by side, keeping the peace with nothing more than the power of her voice. Big Bill grumbled but settled back down.

"Besides, you said you had something for me?" said Marisol.

Big Bill clapped his hands, as if he had only just remembered.

"As a matter of fact, I do."

Bill pulled out the surprise he had tucked under his arm: "Here it is: your favorite fig bush."

Marisol jumped with glee and embraced both Big Bill and the bush. The figs were still attached, and the leaves were battered but clinging.

"That's just about the only thing Joe didn't destroy," said Big Bill. "I uprooted it from the roof of our den and took off running. I said, 'Joe's not getting his lousy hands on my wife's favorite plant.'"

Bill was happy to see it as well—the figs were always rich and juicy, and they made his mother happy. Memories of Cloud Kingdom flooded his brain, taking him back to their old den, the sights and sounds and scents, the cool brush of the air as it swayed the sweet-moss, the color of the light, the spring's reassuring babble as it rushed down the lava and filled the canals.

Marisol broke a fig from its branch and bit in, handing the rest to Bill. He popped the fruit into his mouth and its warm juices triggered another swell of memories, which hit him with such force that he was left with a sorrowful realization: Cloud Kingdom had also been a gift to the Teddycats, and not from another species but from the jungle itself.

"So there's really nothing back there for us?" Bill asked.

"I'm sorry, son," said Big Bill.

"That's something every Teddycat needs to come to peace with," said Bill. "Too many are holding on to an idea of Cloud Kingdom that no longer exists. They need to know it's gone forever, and they need to hear it from you. Otherwise, they might never move on."

"He's right," said Marisol.

Big Bill sighed. "I know it. Just been dreading the task."

"You get cleaned up and composed," said Marisol. "We'll spread the word."

MARISOL CALLED ON the Elders while Bill fetched the younger Teddycats. When they were gathered outside the Garras' den, Big Bill emerged, looking stoic and strong.

"My fellow Teddycats," he began, his voice somehow both grave and soothing. "I was one of the last to leave Cloud Kingdom, and I need to report what I witnessed. Your dens and crops are gone. The Wall burst, and the mountain stream no longer runs through the Kingdom. There is nothing there for us any longer, but we will carry its spirit with us as we move forward together."

Big Bill's words were a blow to the Teddycats' already depleted spirits. Some moaned; others stared off in silent remembrance. Others openly wept.

"There's a chance for a new beginning here in Horizon Cove," said Big Bill, gaining volume and conviction. "We need to reunite, work together, and buckle down, because I don't want to lose another den—or anything else—to Joe."

"We don't like it here," cried Finn the Elder.

"Adjusting to change takes time," said Big Bill. "We're grieving. We've lost loved ones. But let's not lose an entire way of life by bowing to anger and fear and refusing to accept what we know to be the truth. The Teddycats called Horizon Cove home for a long time, and the jungle has decided that we are to return. I think we should listen to the jungle."

"Let's at least return to the trees," said Finn, as others chimed their support and approval.

"Well, funny you should mention that," said Big Bill. "I've been informed that the Pets have plans to help us do just that, so let's show 'em how Teddycats get the job done."

Chapter

THE TEDDYCATS DID their best to sit quietly through a nest-building workshop led by Polly. The Pets typically lived in pendant nests, which hung from the trees, but Polly proposed platform nests, which would most closely mimic Cloud Kingdom: a wide, flat surface suspended high in the air, all the way up at the crown of the tree line. A hush fell over the Teddycats as Polly described the structure. It sounded almost like home, but it would be a huge project, requiring complex materials and assembly. It was all paws and claws on deck.

"We know how to build the nest, but we need your help to install it," said Polly. "With your claws you'll have a much easier time carrying things back and forth."

Bill was impressed by Polly's delivery. There was raw determination in her wobbly eyes. As she explained the various roles and began to assign tasks, Pablo and a couple of the gruffer Pets, Greg and Ray, watched from the side, content to let Polly's vision drive the plan forward. It was handy to have an enforcer, somebody who could bark orders while maintaining an emotional distance. Back in Cloud Kingdom there had been only the Elders, who passed down decrees and then just waited around until the work couldn't be delayed any further. Polly's orders were helpful and maybe even necessary, but they still occasionally bristled Bill's fur. He sat next to Omar and Maia, feeling a bit left out. The shift to Horizon Cove had been so busy, there had hardly been any time to spend with friends. Watching the reunion between his mother and father reminded Bill of the deep affection he held for so many fellow Teddycats, but he felt slightly removed from his friends, still seeking a way back into their routine.

Meanwhile, Maia and Omar were friendlier than ever, finishing each other's sentences and cracking jokes Bill couldn't quite understand. Bill had been secretly jealous of Omar's heroics. He had risked life and limb to distract the humans, allowing for Bill and Elena's escape. Of course, Bill had no shortage of heroics himself, but that mad, noisy dash through the human camp had been just Bill's style, and it pained him that Omar had the chance to pull it off.

"Rotten jackfruit," said Omar.

Maia giggled. "The underside of a monkey's tail."

Omar snorted.

"What are you guys talking about?" whispered Bill. He didn't want to fall even further behind. Polly was explaining the assembly line, and Bill was trying to follow both threads. It was confusing. But Omar and Maia just laughed, as if it was beyond obvious.

Bill felt his face grow hot.

"They're saying the Pets are smelly," whispered Elena, crawling up behind him.

Omar and Maia cracked up, and Polly shot them a glare. They swallowed their laughter and settled down, but Bill felt stung by the encounter. A chill of loneliness swept through him. He narrowed his eyes and focused on the rest of Polly's presentation.

ALL MORNING BILL'S job was to drizzle heaps of mud over bundles of jungle debris. Once dried, the result would serve as the foundation of the Teddycats' new home, strong as wood. But the work was hard, and the mud kept slipping through his grasp. By the time lunch rolled around, Bill was pretty much wiped out, and they had only a few feet finished.

During his break he devoured a pawful of grubs and gnawed on some bark, trying to rip out every last nutrient with his teeth. Pablo ambled over to say hello, and sensed Bill's frustration straightaway.

"Hard work, isn't it?" Pablo chuckled.

"This is going to take forever," said Bill, sighing.

"No, it'll be fine," said Pablo. "And the sooner we have this finished up, the sooner the Pets will be able to leave."

"What if the rains come before we're done?" Bill asked.

"I have faith in you," said Pablo, smiling widely.

"Thanks," said Bill. "I guess I'm just a bit out of it."

"Happens to us all," said Pablo.

"Not me!" shrieked Frank, as he crash-landed between the two.

"Why not team up with Frank?" said Pablo.

"Sure, the buddy system," said Bill. "We could use something like that. But I need somebody with experience and good balance. No offense, Frank."

Pablo was about to defend Frank's sense of equilibrium when Frank abruptly fell over.

"That might be smart," said Pablo.

"None taken," said Frank.

AFTER LUNCH, DIEGO worked alongside Bill, and the hours passed much more quickly and fruitfully. The old scout had a seemingly endless supply of old Teddycat work songs, the very melodies that—by Diego's account, anyway—inspired the construction of Cloud Kingdom. By the time dusk approached, Bill was energized by the sight of what they had accomplished: a small mountain of solid bales, dried to a high gloss, ready to be installed in the sky. Other Teddycats had gathered lengths of vine to be used as a pulley system, and in the morning they would raise them up.

Bill was crusty with dried mud and sweat, his limbs raw with cuts where the sticks had poked and scraped. But the mess felt good—if anybody wanted to know what he'd spent the day doing, they wouldn't need to ask. He was proud of the day's accomplishments and didn't want to see it end, so he took a loopy, long route along the edge of the clearing, back to his parents' new den. In the distance he could hear Frank's happy squawking. Bill smiled. He would miss Frank once the rains began and the Pets set off on their way. There was something about the little Pet that Bill recognized in himself—the spirit of the jungle captured in the rip and run of youth.

"Hey, Garra," said a familiar voice.

Bill turned to face Maia. "Everyone's always sneaking up on me around here!" he said. "What's up, Maia?"

Maia smiled and arched an eyebrow. "Wanna race?"

Chapter

BILL CHASED MAIA into the jungle's humid darkness, and by the time he caught up to her they were deep in the wilderness, lost and laughing. They raced along bumpy branches and swung from vines, catching the rhythm of the forest like a wave. When they reached a king mahogany—a massive hardwood that split the canopy and seemed to almost block the sky—they instinctively began to clamber, each taking a side of the trunk, so that they could see only flashes of the other as the tree stretched and narrowed. Soon the other trees gave way and there were only bugs and birds and a shroud of haze covering the view of Horizon Cove. Bill could see the cliff where he'd met Raffi and the river where they'd fought the crocs. The clearing of the Nest was scrubby and pint-sized but pleasing to see—Bill felt something like a pang upon spotting it for the first time from that height.

If it truly had been a race, then the finish line would have been the very top of the tree, a glittery point in the distance. But instead it was merely an excuse, an invitation to play, and so Bill and Maia each slowed their pace and found a wide notch in which to rest. The jungle spread out before them in a blur of green, mountains reduced to dimples in the landscape. They rested back to back, both breathing heavily.

"Sorry about before," Maia said finally.

"What do you mean?" asked Bill.

"Back at the Nest, with Omar," said Maia. "I didn't mean to push you away."

"I thought it was just a joke," said Bill.

"It was," said Maia. "But I want you to be in on my jokes."

"Me too," said Bill.

Monkeys howled in the distance.

"Must be dinnertime," said Maia.

"How do you like Horizon Cove?" Bill asked.

"It's great," said Maia. But she didn't sound convinced. "I mean, it's fine. I'm getting used to it. Elena loves it."

"I think everyone will be more on board once things calm down," said Bill. "Once we finish the new dens and the Pets get out of our hair."

"Where do you think they go?" Maia asked.

Bill thought about it for a while. "Huh. I'm not sure. Somewhere dry, I guess."

"Weird we'd never seen any Pets before we came to Horizon Cove, then," said Maia.

"Well, it turns out they can hide pretty well."

"That's true," said Maia. "Like, *really* well."

Though they were back to back, Bill could sense Maia's gloomy demeanor. "Does that worry you?" he asked.

Maia sighed. "I'm not sure. We used to take security pretty seriously back in Cloud Kingdom, so I understand why the Pets have these defenses. But I guess I just still don't understand why the Pets bothered to save us from the crocs when they could've kept hiding away."

"Lucky for us, they did," said Bill. "That would've been a hard fight otherwise."

The two sat there in the notch, the bark warm against their fur, as the sun began to set.

"I'm so happy Big Bill's back," said Maia. "Your mom must be just . . . overjoyed."

"That's exactly right," said Bill, laughing.

"What?" Maia asked.

"I'm just picturing my mom, running around with too much joy for once and there's nowhere to put it all."

"You know what I mean," said Maia, digging the blade of her shoulder into Bill's back.

"We should get back," said Bill with a sigh, though a part of him wanted to stay there in the tree with Maia forever.

"Oh, you're right," said Maia, the gloom lifted from her voice.

"Thanks for finding me," said Bill. "I don't know what I'd do here without you."

"Well, if it wasn't for you, I wouldn't be here at all," said Maia.

Bill craned his neck to try to face her. "What do you mean?"

Maia turned as well. "None of us would," she said.

THEY TRUDGED AND wiggled their way back to the Nest, too tired to swing and slide. At slow speeds the jungle took on a different character. It reminded Bill of when he first left Cloud Kingdom, searching for Elena with no clear direction. The forest floor had seemed both shifty and stubborn. Every stone, every fallen tree and tangle of brush had to be beaten back, surpassed, and summitted. The new den would provide a good perch, a more fitting perspective. That was where the Teddycats were meant to be, up in the sky. It was where they belonged. Bill was determined that they could be of the jungle while still maintaining their natural habitat. The best of both worlds: That's what they deserved. Bill smiled to himself as he followed Maia through a hollow trunk that opened into a tumble of moss, and they laughed as they rolled down the soft hill at the other end. When they returned to the path at the edge of the clearing, they looked up to find the slanting light filling the nests like lanterns. To Bill it felt like an oasis.

The peace lasted only a moment, as the first Teddycat to cross them on the path was Omar. He seemed lost and agitated, and when he spotted Bill and Maia he tried to smile but the result was crooked and weak.

"Hey, Omar," Bill chirped. "You eat yet?"

"No," said Omar. "Did you?"

"Just getting back from an evening stroll," said Bill.

"Everything cool, O?" Maia asked.

"Hm? Sorry, everything's fine," said Omar. "I just realized I have to get back to my den."

"Well, we're headed that way," said Maia. "Let's roll together."

Bill tried to catch Maia's eye. It was clear that Omar was miffed or otherwise out of sorts and would be better off alone with his thoughts. Bill could recognize seething anger better than almost anyone—back in Cloud Kingdom, Big Bill was always riled up about something, either lagging infrastructure projects, bickering Elders, or Bill's latest misadventure—but Maia was already pushing the group forward as the silence between them began to gnaw, and Bill knew when it finally broke it wouldn't be a pretty scene.

They rounded the corner, and the Nest rose before them. Pets and Teddycats milled about, preparing dinner or bathing.

"Remember that nutty coati that came to Cloud Kingdom?" Omar asked.

"Ugh, gross," spat Maia. "Why'd you have to bring that up?"

"Norm," said Bill. "His name was Norm."

Norm had been brought to Cloud Kingdom to recover under the care of nurses like Bill's mother, but his condition only seemed to worsen. Marisol invited him to stay with the Garras, hoping that a family environment and schedule would calm his rattled nerves. Bill remembered Norm jolting awake in the middle of the night, screaming in panic and pain, throwing himself around the den until Big Bill and Marisol held him tight.

"Oh man," said Omar, "remember how bad that thing smelled?"

"He was sick," Bill snarled. "He couldn't take care of himself."

"Why're you bringing this up, Omar?" Maia asked.

"I was just trying to figure out what these birds smell like, and I suddenly realized they stink like that stupid coati," Omar said.

"You're better than this," said Maia. "Don't lash out at Bill."

"What?" said Omar. "I know it's been bothering you, too. But I guess because Bill's here we can't talk about anything."

"That's not true!" said Maia.

Surrounding Pets and Teddycats began to take notice of the bickering trio.

"Not now," said Bill, grimacing. "Not here."

"I can do whatever I want," said Omar. "You're not an Elder, Bill Garra. You can't boss me around. Sometimes I wonder whether we should have left you in the clutches of the humans."

Maia gasped. Bill rushed up to Omar, until their snouts almost touched.

"Oh, I'm not an Elder?" shouted Bill. "Well, you're not my friend. Why don't you get lost, Omar? And don't come back!"

A small flock of Pets intervened, separating Bill from Omar. Sally, a friendly Pet with a perky tail, flashed her lopsided smile and whisked Omar away.

"Omar, come with me," said Sally. "I've been dying to show you something."

Bill was fuming mad, but Maia just seemed hurt and confused. He tried to comfort her.

"I'm sorry, Maia," he said. "I didn't mean for that to happen."

"We're all friends," said Maia. "What keeps pulling us apart?"

Bill shook his head. "After what Omar and I went through, I figured we were buds for life."

Frank was among the Pets attracted by the scuffle.

"We'll take care of him for ya!" said Frank.

"Thanks," said Bill. It wasn't until later that night, curled up in his nest, that he realized he had no idea what Frank meant by that.

Chapter

14

THE NEXT MORNING Bill woke to a rushing wind clattering everything in the clearing. It was the first sign—the rains were close. Bill leapt up and poked his head out of the nest, and the wind immediately stung his eyes. He retreated back into his shelter, which leaned slightly with each gust. Bill shook his head and tried again with one paw resting on his snout for protection. The wind swept the entire Cove with an eerie whistle.

Bill cautiously climbed out of the den and took refuge in some tall grass, but it was blown nearly horizontal. The trees swayed and the palm fronds shook. Fruit and nuts dropped, landing with a thud. Bill expected to see the Pets rejoicing or even preparing for departure.

This was their big day! But the few already moving about the clearing seemed to barely take note, despite their ruffled feathers and the general disarray.

Bill spotted Maia through the gathering as water filled his eyes. He shouted her name, but it was lost to the wind. He jumped and waved until she noticed, and they each slowly made their way to the middle of the clearing, where the wildflowers were losing petals to the gale. Some were almost stripped, their bare stems stark reminders of their beauty and frailty. Bill spun around, getting his bearings. It felt like the whole place was about to be ripped out of the ground and flung from the jungle. The roar of the wind filled his ears. He was afraid it might blow right through his head. Bill had seen a lot of things in his life—he'd fallen over a waterfall, been taken prisoner by humans—but this wind was something new. It was raw and uncaring, with no motive or direction.

"This is crazy!" said Maia when they finally managed to get within shouting distance.

"I know!" yelled Bill, the wind stealing the words right out of his mouth. "But at least the Pets will be on their way out now."

"That's true," said Maia. "Though they don't really seem to be in that big of a rush."

"I noticed," said Bill. "Maybe they're so organized, there's just no need for a final push."

"Teddycats wouldn't know anything about that," said Maia, smiling.

"We're not great at change," said Bill. "But we're making it work."

"I guess we'll have to just see what happens," said Maia. "But if they don't start packing up soon, I'd ask Pablo."

"I'll keep my eyes open," said Bill. A huge gust blew into the clearing. Bill thought the whole world might turn upside down. "So long as they don't get blown out of my head."

"Seriously!" shouted Maia. "Stay safe! I'm going to check on Elena."

Bill figured his parents had to be up—the noise was almost unbearable as wind screamed through the trees—and they could weigh in on the Pets' impending departure. He didn't want to undermine or second-guess his hosts and neighbors, but in the interest of long-term relationships, it felt important for everyone to be of the same mind and working together.

Bill was starting to get the hang of moving about in heavy winds: low to the ground, eyes open just a sliver, gripping the grass tightly with his paws, using his claws as anchors. He noticed Pets eyeing his technique with approval. This was the kind of flexibility Bill knew the Teddycats were capable of, adapting their skills to break into the wider jungle.

Pablo dropped down beside Bill. It was odd—if anything, Pablo's flight was smoother in the storm than it had been any other time. Bill shrugged. The Pets were weird animals. It probably *would* take a walloping wind to straighten out their bumps and curves.

"Morning, Mr. Garra," said Pablo. While Bill and Maia had to shout to be heard, the Pets' cloying chirps were able to withstand—even slice through—the gusts with impressive force.

"Mornin'," said Bill. He could see his parents stirring in their nest, strapping down anything loose on the floor. "You guys must be excited. Time to start the Great Migration."

"Whoa, hold on there," said Pablo. "The wind's arrival is certainly noted, but we're not out the door yet. Lots to do here first."

Bill bit his lip. "Won't that put you behind schedule?"

"Look," said Pablo, wings ruffling in the wind, "I'm sorry to say it, but based on yesterday's performance, we just don't think the Teddycats are ready to take over the Nest."

The muscles of Bill's shoulders, still sore from the previous day's labors, begged to differ. But Pablo's scold left Bill feeling small and ashamed. Maybe the Teddycats *weren't* ready. What would happen if the crocs came back? Or Joe? Or any other bad-tempered apex predator? With a potential mass migration of Olingos on their way, Bill had to be sure they were prepared for anything. He vowed to do better. Whatever it took.

"I'm sorry," said Bill, as Pablo began to stalk away. "We'll work harder."

He wasn't sure Pablo had even heard him above the wind, but the Pet turned his long neck and delivered a steely smirk.

BIG BILL DID not take the news well. "The wind's here, they're out. That was the deal," he said. "How do they expect us to trust them if we're getting dipped and spun all over the place?"

"It might be best if the Elders didn't hear about this straightaway," said Marisol.

Bill had to agree. It was hard enough to explain the Pets' position to his father, much less the Teddycats who had been all but cheering for him to fail.

"We'll keep it mum until we figure out what we need to do," said Big Bill.

"Garras, I see the breeze picked up."

They all turned, and there was Diego, filling the entrance to the den.

"Time for these birds to fly," said Diego.

"Indeed," said Big Bill.

"They just want to be sure we're ready," said Bill. "They're doing us a favor, really."

"Let's really put our backs into it today, boys," said Big Bill. "Give 'em no choice but to bow down to the Teddycats."

"In a friendly, supportive way," said Marisol.

"Of course," said Big Bill, blowing his wife a kiss.

"Wouldn't do it any other way, mate," said Diego.

"These guys," said Marisol, shaking her head.

Bill yelped in frustration.

"Settle down, settle down," cooed Marisol.

"We need the Pets to trust us!" Bill hollered.

"Jeez, tiny place you got here," said Diego, looking around as dust swirled in the den and intense puffs whipped outside.

The Garras closed ranks around Bill, who appeared to be on the verge of tears.

"Well, guess I'll see ya down at the site," said Diego.

"Don't cry," comforted Marisol, once Diego took his leave.

"I'm not crying!" Bill insisted. "I think my eyes are just tired from all the wind."

"This wind has everybody out of sorts," said Marisol. "But let's not get ahead of ourselves."

"Listen to your mother," said Big Bill.

"This is for you too, Bill," said Marisol. "Our little kitten has been keeping this community together with nothing but grit and swallowed pride. Between the Elders, the elements, and these blasted birds, he hasn't had a proper meal or solid stretch of rest since we got here."

Big Bill seemed slightly chastened.

"As for you," continued Marisol, "you're coming off a long journey! You're tired! You're frustrated! Things are changing!"

"I just don't want to take it out on the Pets," said Bill. "I want them to believe in us, because I believe in them."

As if on cue, Frank drifted past the den. "Howdy!" he shouted. "Li'l windy! Woo!"

A forceful gust bent the trees, and Bill watched as all his hard work rattled in the leaves. He knew they had to act fast to secure everything.

"Hey, Frank," said Bill, "wait for me!"

Chapter 15

BILL AND DIEGO were high in the trees. The winds had calmed, though an occasional gust still sent everything sideways and swaying. But Pablo had determined it was safe, and so Bill climbed up into the trees to make sure everything was still fastened into place, and asked other Teddycats to do the same. Diego had resisted at first but, perhaps remembering Bill's frustrations back at the Garra den, had chosen to go along. But Bill would have gone up into the trees no matter how violent the wind. For him, the benefits of another hard day's work were as clear as could be: A finished dwelling might persuade the Pets that the Nest would be well cared for and encourage them to pack up and shove off as soon as possible.

Plus, Frank was in the trees, and Pablo was watching, and the Elders needed to see progress so they might sooner accept Horizon Cove as their home. There was a lot to do, and even if Bill got it all done, he knew he could never make everybody happy.

The task before them was rather brutal, but they soon lost track of time. It also freed up the conversation. Speaking required additional energy, so Bill was choosy with his words and dove right into the deep stuff.

"You've known my dad for a long time," Bill began.

He had always been curious about the relationship between the old scout and Big Bill.

Diego grunted.

"Longer than me, anyways."

"Watch what you're doin'—you're getting the gunk all over."

Some mud had slid from the bundled plank as the two tried to position it securely between the nooks of the upper canopy, but Bill figured Diego's warning to be mostly a diversion from the talk he was determined to have sooner or later. He knew that Big Bill and Diego had taken several lengthy scouting trips together, including a few different expulsions, when errant Teddycats were forced out of Cloud Kingdom after committing terrible acts or putting the community at risk. The Elders would vote, and if the offense was grave enough, the Teddycat was expelled. Scouts and security experts would accompany the expelled Teddycat out of Cloud Kingdom and down to the jungle floor, then deep into the wilderness, days and days away from Cloud Kingdom, so there would be no way for the expelled to find their way back.

Everybody in Cloud Kingdom knew when a Teddycat would be expelled. It did not happen often. But the idea had always captivated younger Teddycats, who couldn't yet see the punishment for what it was: a near-certain death sentence.

Once, Bill had seen banishments as a sort of dark freedom, a chance to break away from the safe yet sometimes stifling Kingdom. But that was before he had truly seen the jungle, before he had undertaken the mission to save Elena and the Teddycats from the humans. That was the first time he had skirted out onto a limb that he wasn't sure could hold him. Previous trips into the jungle were alive with a mischievous intensity, but truthfully the stakes were low: Bill always knew he could return to the Kingdom at the end of the day, so he felt no need to compromise or adapt, no matter what the jungle threw at him.

Bill tidied up the mud and tried again. "What was my dad like, out on the prowl?"

Diego groaned but seemed resigned to the conversation. "You know your pop," he said.

"Just give me *something*," Bill begged. "He never tells me anything about the old days."

"That's 'cause it's not for kittens, mate!" growled Diego.

"I'm not a kitten anymore!" shouted Bill, pounding his chest in frustration.

"I know you ain't," said Diego, sighing, "but some of these stories aren't pretty."

"I need to hear them," said Bill. "I need to know how bad things can get, and I need to know that we have faced down evil and survived before."

Diego fell silent, and Bill tried to concentrate on the job. The tree had three main arteries, and they were attempting to bridge the gap between them with their mud-hewn stick bundles. It was arduous and dangerous work. Bill could feel the Pets and the Elders watching him from below, squinting and craning to get a glimpse of any possible issues.

"It's not my decision," said Diego.

"I'm sorry," said Bill. "I'm just nervous about everything happening down on the ground. I think I might be taking it out on you."

"Relax," said Diego. "You're up in the trees now. They can't get you here."

"Wanna bet?" said Bill, laughing.

"Well, most of them, anyways," said Diego. "Besides, you can't worry about keeping others happy. That's up to them. Your job, besides making sure I don't fall out of this tree, is to do the right thing and treat others fairly. And from what I've seen, I don't think you need much help with that."

"We have been through a lot, haven't we?" said Bill.

"We sure have, kid," said Diego. "So no need to worry about me and your pa. That was ages ago. Ancient history. We have new tales to tell, new destinies to discover."

"Thanks, Diego."

The old scout stretched his back and peered down at the ground. "Back to work, mate. Need these wonky birds off my back, pronto."

"You got it."

BILL WORKED THROUGH lunch, even after Diego gave up and inched his way down the trunk to refuel. He didn't want to so much as make eye contact with anybody who might have lingering doubts about the Teddycats' future in the Nest. But once Diego departed, Bill took a moment to digest the view from his high vantage point. The rolling green of the jungle was visible only between shreds of low clouds that had been deposited by the wind that had only recently slowed, and a valley in the near distance was shrouded completely. Bill felt a pang of homesickness but brushed it off with a shrug and returned to his duties.

If the mud dried too quickly, the nest-building materials wouldn't latch securely to the tree limbs or remain reliably steady as time went on and the elements of the wilderness had their way. The jungle changed quickly, raging against itself in an endless loop of self-destruction and renewal. That's why Cloud Kingdom had always felt like a dream: Removed from this type of chaos, life slowed down.

Bill kept the mud wet and pliable all through Diego's lunch and ensuing siesta. He let his mind wander as he stirred. They were only assembling the foundation, but he could already imagine the new den: a network of sanctuaries high in the trees, the best of Cloud Kingdom without the sense of total removal. Bill envisioned his parents growing old together in a peaceful hideaway. He saw huddles of Elders happy to sing Bill's praises; he saw Maia and Elena as contributing members of the jungle; and he saw Luke and his family integrated throughout the community, in a triumphant return to the age-old Teddycat and Olingo alliance.

A lonely yet brisk gust of wind swept Bill into the corner of the crook where he was stationed. A rogue, Bill figured. A leftover from the morning's storm. He reassembled his materials and got back to work, a bit shaky but appreciative of the reminder to keep his wits about him.

"I'm comin' up," hollered Diego. Bill glanced down. The scout was about halfway up the tree, just before a long stretch of exposed trunk. It looked to Bill like the middle of the tree had been shorn of everything but its bark. In some places even the bark was gone, leaving only raw patches of bare wood.

"Take your time," yelled Bill. He was looking forward to razzing his partner about the long break. Diego, for all his tenacity and toughness, worked in a slower register than Bill. Of course, he was many years older, but Bill would still need to remind him of the productivity gap, especially since Diego had so gruffly reprimanded him over the supposedly spilled mud.

"Gonna show you how it's done," Diego shouted. "Just you wait."

"Oh, I've been waiting," said Bill, laughing. "Ever since—"

Suddenly, a burst of wind hit Bill like an uppercut, knocking him over. As soon as he had his claws dug into the tree, he looked out into the distance—the clouds moved, allowing glimpses of blue sky and green jungle. The winds had returned, and Bill and Diego were right in their path.

Bill scurried to the closest downward-facing limb to make sure Diego had withstood the blast. At first Bill couldn't see him, but then Diego swung back into view. He was dangling by a single claw, his body rippling in the wind. Bill watched helplessly as Diego fought for traction, but with nothing but the trunk to dig into, there was no protection and no safety net. Cries rose up from the ground as bystanders caught sight of Diego's predicament. Some words were lost to the wind but others reached Bill, who was still grappling with the severity of the situation.

As far as he could tell, there were two options: They could launch a rescue mission from the ground or from above. It seemed unlikely that Diego could recover his balance. The wind was just too strong. And if Bill crept down to try to grab Diego, they could both be goners. Help would have to come from below.

Bill stabbed his claws into the tree and twisted his body around until he found the best possible view of

Diego while still securely attached to the tree. He didn't want to tumble down the tree and latch on to Diego, adding more weight and dragging them both farther down.

"Diego!" cried Bill. "Hold on, the Pets will come for you."

Bill hoped that was true. It was the safest and most plausible solution. When the Pets had saved the Teddycats from the crocs, there had been no warning, just a sudden shriek, and then the claws nabbed them by the neck.

The gusts were wicked and relentless. Whenever Bill opened his mouth to cry for help or reassure Diego, he was immediately choked by harsh, heavy wind. Bill could taste the jungle, everything that had been stripped and kicked up, pushed along and mixed together. His eyes burned, his mind rattled, and his limbs shook as his claws pried into the wood.

"Stick to it!" cried Bill. "They're coming!"

He couldn't imagine a world without Diego. He was a permanent fixture, a constant. But of course Bill knew that wasn't true. He had learned that in the desert, experienced death firsthand, seen it up close. It hadn't felt real then, either. The future forked into two, and one was almost impossible to picture.

They were too far from the other trees to jump, and there were no vines to climb down or swing from. Each time the wind went slack and Bill dared to hope that the storm had passed, it started all over again. He could hear Diego's howls ringing in the current. They were more regretful than curdling, but Bill knew that they had the potential to haunt him for years.

From Bill's perch, the clearing looked small, an inconsequential spot within an imposing ocean of treetops. There was no way to tell if anyone on the ground was any closer to making a move. His throat was hoarse, his heart sore with panic.

Bill had waited long enough. He puffed himself up and plotted his way down the trunk, eyes closed, envisioning the plan. There was a cluster of branches just above the shorn section. If he could reach those, there might be a way to guide Diego back to safety. It was risky and dangerous, with slim hopes for success. But it was time to act. He took a deep breath and unhooked a front claw, ready to dash.

To reach the trunk he had to swing under the crook, leaving himself completely vulnerable to the elements. On the way up it had been so simple, an afterthought. Now it felt shocking and perilous—the ground was a long way down.

"I'm coming for you, Diego!" hollered Bill. He knew there was no way the scout could hear him. It was more a reminder to himself of the scale of the moment—the stakes. Even though his throat was hoarse and gritty and his voice was shot, he gave a whooping war cry and leapt off the crook, hind legs fully extended, claws set to lance the first thing they touched.

Chapter 16

BILL'S SPLIT SECOND of free fall, before Pablo swooped him under his wing, felt like a lifetime. It was an entire existence between life and death, a terrifying limbo that had Bill's mind racing and lungs burning by the time Pablo landed on the grass and released him. Bill rolled on the grass, frantic, searching for Diego, until Pablo turned and unloaded the scout from his other wing.

Diego was pale and shaken, his fur shooting in every direction. He hacked and gagged, staggering away from the small gathering of Teddycats and Pets. Bill couldn't read his expression—it was somewhere between hatred and shock. Diego collapsed over a stump, his ribs visible with each sharp intake of breath. Slowly, Bill approached him.

"Diego, are you all right?"

Bill hadn't even noticed that the storm had passed until he felt his mouth. His snout was raw, burned from the wind. Sunlight began to emerge from the sky's gray grip. Diego turned to face Bill. His eyes were wide and his smile flat.

"Are you okay?" Bill asked.

"Help me up, mate," said Diego.

Bill happily obliged, yanking his friend up with almost too much gusto.

"Slow down," yelped Diego. "Easy does it."

"Sorry, sorry," stuttered Bill. "Just happy to have you here, safe and sound."

But Diego brushed Bill aside. "You!" he shouted, shaking a fist at Pablo.

Pablo turned to face him.

"Yeah, you!" Diego sneered.

Bill jumped between them, desperate to stop a fight. If Diego turned on Pablo and the Pets, there was no telling who would join him. It would fracture the entire Teddy-cat community and galvanize the grumbling Elders. But

Diego again pushed him aside. Bill was surprised by the old scout's brute strength, built and trained over many years of faithful, selfless service. The Pets and Teddycats formed a half circle around the unfolding scene, and the air was thick with an edgy and unpredictable energy.

"Yes?" said Pablo, slowly, his wings shuddering.

"Get over here!" cried Diego. "You big, fat, beautiful lug!"

They embraced, and the clearing filled with cheers. Bill sighed with relief. Diego was safe, and peace still reigned in Horizon Cove.

Bill's smile was so wide it ached.

"Look out!" shouted Frank. Everybody scooted over and looked to the sky, as hunks of sticks and dried mud rained down from the canopy and hit the grass with a splatter. "Dang, that was a close one."

Bill was so relieved that Diego was safe he didn't want to ask Pablo why the Pets had encouraged the Teddycats to climb the trees even though the winds hadn't passed. Of course the wind was liable to blow any which way at any given time, and nobody could ever know what it might do, but the fact remained that they had risked their lives by taking to the trees to build a project designed and commissioned by the Pets. Where

Bill came from, if a near disaster unfolded on your watch, that was your disaster. But he couldn't help but feel as if the Teddycats would get stuck with this one as well.

"Close call," said Pablo, neck craned toward the sky.

"Crazy wind," said Polly, joining his side.

"I'm taking the rest of the day, mate," said Diego.

"You've earned it," said Bill. "Besides, we have got to redesign our whole approach to this new den. If a windstorm can whip up these kinds of problems, we need a better solution."

Pablo laughed. The energy shifted back from celebratory to unease. "It's a bump in the road. A hiccup. Abandoning the project now would be a huge mistake, not to mention a waste of time for both the Teddycats and the Pets. I can tell you now that we will not be able to start our migration if construction is still in flux."

Bill's snout burned in frustration. Had Pablo not seen what had almost just transpired? Diego's panicked eyes, tail stiff with wind, would haunt Bill's dreams for a long time to come. But he had to be practical. Lashing out at Pablo wouldn't accomplish anything and would likely only drive the Teddycats further away from their goal of establishing a safe, comfortable, and vibrant habitat.

"You're right," said Bill through clenched teeth.

Pablo nodded. A bit smugly, Bill thought. Diego was already well on his way back to his den, and he wondered what thoughts and regrets had passed through the old scout's mind as he dangled in thin air.

The crowd began to disperse. Pablo and Polly were chatting, rolling their eyes at some unknown party. Bill started the process of cleaning up the mud and sticks. The platform had broken apart as it fell, and there was much more of it than he would have expected. It covered a good stretch of the lower end of the clearing. The work was slow and maddening, almost making Bill miss the excitement of the canopy.

"Look out!" someone cried.

Instinctively, Bill glanced up. He figured more mud was on its way down. Instead, an entire tree was swaying. Bill stumbled backward, twisting his head to see who else might be caught in the trunk's downward path. There was Elena, playing with fallen sticks.

Bill raced toward her, and as he did a loud, sickening crack splintered the jungle din, followed by a steadily rising whoosh. The tree was falling. The storm had cracked its core. Nobody had noticed amid the excitement. The leaves whistled as they fell through the air, mimicking the wind, and Bill felt the tree's huge presence bear down on him. A shadow spread. It was surprisingly

cold. Soon Elena was squirming in his arms. Bill still couldn't muster the courage to look up, but perhaps that was good—it surely would have slowed him down. There must have been shouts and pleas coming from the crowd, but all Bill could hear was the falling tree and the beating of his own heart.

Chapter

17

ELENA SQUIRMED OUT of Bill's grasp. He let her go and she sprinted in manic circles for a moment, burning off any lingering fear. The crowd's cries and shouts were audible again, though Bill's blood still hummed in his ears. Before him lay the powerful tree, the same one he had just climbed. A heavy branch had landed just inches from his hind legs. Another second and the two of them would have been flattened.

"Is everybody okay?" Bill asked.

Nobody seemed to know. The tree was so huge, even on its side, that it would take the whole afternoon to rustle through its foliage. Bill's heart was racing. His chest burned with each breath. He threw back his head and took deep gulps of air through his snout. He felt grounded to the forest floor in a way he had never before. At that moment he wasn't sure if he would ever climb again.

Elena approached, somewhat shyly. "You saved me, Bill," she said.

"Again!" said Maia.

"Oh, hey," said Bill. "Where'd you come from, Maia?"

"We almost got hit by the tree," said Elena, pointing.

"I know," said Maia. Bill could tell she was trying not to cry. "Let's go back to the den, what do you say? Get cleaned up."

"Can Bill come with us?" Elena asked.

"Of course!" said Maia, turning to Bill. "We would love that, wouldn't we?"

Bill cracked a tired smile. "No place I'd rather be."

BILL SLUMPED AGAINST the wall of Maia's den. It was sparse but snug, warm with affection. Bill was running hot as well. The quick succession of near disasters had him rattled. He tried to let his mind run free, away from visions of Diego's death and Elena lost under the tree. He had to focus on the positives: his father's return, the impending departure of the Pets, the fact that Diego and Elena were still alive and mostly well. But it was difficult to hold on to these triumphs. Whenever Bill thought he was safely removed from danger, he heard that tree and felt that shadow overtake him.

Thankfully, it appeared Elena had escaped significant injury. A few scrapes and some lingering shock, but Bill doubted she understood the sheer size of the tree or the pain and damage it came so close to causing. Elena was young but had already been through so much—capture by the humans, the destruction of her home, near death at the hands of the crocs—that Bill could only hope she would be bolstered by these experiences rather than haunted by them.

"Let's all just take a moment to breathe," said Maia in a soothing voice. Bill was surprised to find himself on the verge of tears. He was grateful for the chance to recuperate away from the prying eyes of his parents and the Pets. All he wanted was a few moments of peace with his friends.

"I think I want to go back to Cloud Kingdom," said Elena matter-of-factly.

Bill and Maia exchanged a glance, then they both broke out laughing.

"What?" cried Elena. "I wanna!"

"I know, sweets," said Maia. "We're not laughing at you."

"The opposite, actually!" said Bill, still giggling. "We're happy you said it."

"That way we don't have to," Maia said.

"You guys want to go back, too?" Elena asked between sniffles.

Bill and Maia's eyes met again, and this time they lingered. Maia nodded. This question was Bill's to answer.

"We miss Cloud Kingdom, sure," Bill said. "But this is our new home. And while it might not look like much right now . . ."

"It smells bad, and trees are falling down!" said Elena.

"Exactly," said Bill. "That wind you felt, the same wind that blew over that tree, is going to bring lots of changes, and I think most of them will be good."

"But, Bill, when you found me in a cage with the humans, you said we were going home. Why aren't we there? What happened to Cloud Kingdom?" Elena asked, biting her lip.

If it had been any other kitten, Bill would have shrouded the truth. But Elena was a fighter. She knew Joe and the humans better than almost any other Teddy-cat.

"The humans found it," said Bill.

"Oh no," said Elena. She exhaled thoughtfully. "But Cloud Kingdom was the safest place in the whole jungle. If Joe found us there, he can find us anywhere."

"That's not true," said Maia. "The Pets have figured out all sorts of secret, clever ways to hide that they are sharing with us."

"I don't want to hide anymore," said Elena.

"Me neither," said Bill.

Something about Elena's sad, simple statement stuck in Bill's mind for the rest of the evening. The sun set—same as every other day, no matter the turbulence—which was both a relief and a reminder of how small the Teddycats were in the face of the jungle's grand chaos. He shared Elena's desire to exist in the jungle just as they were, without fear of discovery or destruction. But it seemed only the humans had that privilege. And what good did it do them? They ransacked the forest, destroyed lives and families, all for something they didn't need and hardly understood.

What would a human do with a claw? Bill didn't understand. And yet he wondered if the Teddycats would act the same way if given the opportunity, or if they would resist the temptation to re-create the jungle as they saw fit, no matter the cost.

Chapter

18

DESPITE A WEEK'S worth of wind, the Pets still remained in Horizon Cove, seemingly no closer to packing up and moving on. It was a sensitive subject around the clearing, and Bill could sense the other Teddycats' rising frustration as each morning Pablo presented a new plan for the Teddycats' den in the trees. While some of them sounded reasonable to Bill (if attempted outside the windy season), he couldn't help but feel that the Teddycats would be better suited to design their own habitat. To make matters worse, Pablo was treating the Pets' lingering residence as a favor to the Teddycats, which Bill had a hard time accepting. The Teddycats were a proud species, and the Elders especially would chafe at the suggestion that the Pets knew what was best for them, even if they *had* saved their lives and handed them a place to live.

A part of Bill wanted the rains to arrive early and drench the Pets, punishing them for their failure to act. If the Teddycats were going to re-create the sense of safety and community they had enjoyed in Cloud Kingdom, they had to do the work on their own. But how could Bill evict the Pets from their own home while still appearing grateful for all they had done? It was a fine line to tread, and it grew even finer every day.

IT WAS ANOTHER bright jungle morning. The winds carried all manner of shrieks and hisses, mating calls, and battle cries. Bill was hiding out in his den, resting his muscles while trying to avoid Pablo and the Pets. The night before they had finally finished breaking down, chopping up, and carting off the lumber from the fallen tree.

Bill's claw was gunky with sap, and his spirits sagged. Whenever he thought of that tree he felt a rush of panic, remembering the shadow falling hard and fast down on Elena. Trees fell every day in the jungle. It was part of the life cycle. The forest rewarded the trees that fought the hardest for sunlight. But as Bill knew, anything climbing that high left a lot of itself vulnerable to both predator attack and the bite of the elements.

Mr. and Mrs. Garra were out on a stroll around the clearing. For Bill, watching them together was one of Horizon Cove's greatest pleasures. They seemed closer than ever. The pressures of Cloud Kingdom—his father's political career and his mother's nursing efforts—had aged them prematurely. Now they strolled the clearing like newlyweds, holding paws and smelling flowers. It gave Bill hope to see them so happy. No matter where or how the Teddycats settled, life would continue.

A voice broke through Bill's grumpy fog. "This place looks weird." Bill shot up—it was Luke, back with the Olingos! Finally, his friend had returned, and with reinforcements!

Bill stuck his head out of the den, wagging his tongue back and forth in excitement. And there was Luke, looking a bit worse for wear and all alone.

"Where's everybody else?" asked Bill.

"Well, nice to see you too!" said Luke, through a wounded scowl.

"I'm sorry!" said Bill, slapping his head. "That's not how I meant it. I was just surprised. But you're back! I'm so glad."

"Oh, I'm back, all right," said Luke. His smile was back too, and the sight of it made Bill happy all over again. "Made record time, too. You shoulda seen me racin' through the jungle, through snakes and quicksand and a few close calls with Joe, if you can believe it . . ."

"We had a Joe scare ourselves," said Bill. "Oh, and guess what? My dad's back!"

"Big Bill?" Luke asked, suddenly straight-backed and alert. "How's he doing?"

"Don't worry," said Bill, realizing that Luke knew his father only from what Bill had shared, which back in the day had usually been punishment-related. "He's different here than he was back in Cloud Kingdom. Not as fiery and intense."

"Yeah, this place seems to really have an effect on people," murmured Luke.

"What do you mean?"

"Nothing," said Luke, shaking his head. "Just, it's weird to be back here. Good, but weird. And why are the Pets still hanging around?"

"Don't get me started," said Bill, rolling his eyes. "Hey, tell me about the Olingos! What happened with your parents? Wait—you must be starving. You want some grubs? Water?"

"Both, please," said Luke, rubbing his belly.

ONCE LUKE FINISHED his meal and got settled in the Garras' den, Bill asked again about the rest of the Olingos.

"Sorry to report," said Luke, "the Olingos do not share the Teddycats' excitement over a return to Horizon Cove. They're staying put. I'm sorry, Bill. I did what I could."

"I know you did," said Bill. "I'm sorry you went all that way for nothing."

"It wasn't for nothing," said Luke. "I learned a lot. I tested myself. I feel strong."

"That's great," said Bill, unsure of how to tell his friend that he had been feeling a bit differently. Throughout the history of their friendship, Bill had been the one charging forward, taking risks, and fancying himself a true jungle soul. But with his spirit and strength sapped by the twin near disasters of Elena and Diego *and* the Pets' mystifying reluctance to leave despite every indication that the rains were due, Bill had to admit that his Olingo friend was now the more swashbuckling of the two. Bill was even envious of Luke's scratches—proof of his adventures—and he listened raptly as Luke described the incidents behind each one.

"Hopped a hippo here," said Luke, pointing to a jagged slice to his shoulder. "Almost got trampled by a herd of pronghorns. And *then* I slid through that quicksand I might've mentioned . . ."

"You did mention that," said Bill. "What does quicksand feel like?"

"Not bad," said Luke. "Just a little goopy."

"Probably gets worse the longer you're stuck," said Bill.

"I'd expect so," said Luke, yawning.

"Tuckered out from the trip?" Bill asked.

"Just a tad," said Luke. "This was the biggest meal I've had in a while."

"Relax and digest," said Bill. "But then tell me about your parents!"

Bill missed Doris and Freddy, whom he had come to know and respect during his first trip into the wild. While he continued to hope that the Olingos would someday accept his offer and move to Horizon Cove, their stubborn insistence on grinding out a shaky existence amid the chaos of the jungle inspired him.

"Oh, the usual," said Luke. "You know them. Dad says this side of the jungle gets bad light, which leads to less food, or less flavorful, anyway."

"Huh," said Bill. "I've never heard that before."

"Well, he seems pretty sure of it."

Luke yawned again. He glanced about the clearing and shuddered a bit.

"So what do you want to do now that you're back?" Bill asked. "We've been working on a few projects."

"Who do you mean, 'we'?" asked Luke. "You and the Pets?"

"Pretty much," said Bill. "We've, uh, there have been some setbacks."

"I'll say!" said Luke. "For starters, the place looks weird."

"You mentioned that," said Bill. "Weird like how?"

"I can't quite explain it," said Luke, scratching his wrinkled snout. "But it's definitely different than it was when I left. Are the Pets treating you fine?"

"Of course," said Bill. "Better than fine. Does it look different? Is that what you mean? Because a tree did just come down."

"It's more of a feeling," said Luke. "Which tree fell?"

They dropped from the Garra den down to the clearing to get a better view of the fresh gap in the canopy, and Bill told Luke the story of his brush with death.

"That was a scary moment," said Bill. "It's just, everything's been a bit rushed. We're trying to finish up construction quickly so the Pets can get out of here before the rains."

Luke spun around, head cocked sideways and eyes almost crossed in surprise. "If the Pets want to beat the rainy season they'd better hustle. Trust me, I was out in the jungle, and the migrations are well under way. Everything from birds to snakes is already on the move. If the Pets are serious about beating the rains, they're the last ones out."

Bill chewed his lip thoughtfully. "They're helping us," he said finally. "We owe them our lives. Are they a bit odd? Sure, of course they are. But the Teddycats were considered weird, even mythical, and we all know the truth behind that."

"Teddycats *are* weird," said Luke, a grin spreading across his face. "Everyone knows that. But whatever you say. Now, if you don't mind, I'm gonna grab some more grub."

"Help yourself," said Bill. "Then I need to introduce you to somebody."

Chapter

WHEN BILL AND Luke found Frank he was squawking and hollering as usual, trying to muster up enough liftoff to knock a cluster of jackfruit from its towering tree.

"Got a hankering for 'em something fierce," said Frank. "Wings flappin' in the breeze, you know. That'll really work up an appetite."

"It has been breezy," agreed Bill. "Frank, this is my good buddy Luke. He's been out on a mission, back to the Olingo den. How about I leave you guys to chat and get to know each other while I scamper up that jack trunk and get us some fruit?"

"Sounds good," said Frank. "Any friend of Bill's . . ."

"I could eat," said Luke.

Bill bared his claws and ripped his way up to the crown of the jackfruit tree. The whole chore should have taken only a few seconds, tops, but he wanted to leave his friends alone for a bit longer. He knew that Luke—because of the historically harsh treatment of Olingos—was slow to embrace a different species. So Bill made a big show of sawing the jackfruit stems at their widest point and shaking the fronds to make his mission seem more dramatic. He wanted Luke to have plenty of time to bask in Frank's nutty presence, especially if he was still feeling down from his journey and the Olingos' decision to stay.

When he returned to the ground, Frank and Luke were craning their necks up at the tree, jaws slack and arms crossed.

"Getting along?" asked Bill. "What're you guys talking about?"

"Mostly we talked about how hungry we are," said Luke.

"Pretty much!" said Frank.

"What did I say? Loads in common already," said Bill, cracking the jackfruit against his knee. "Now let's eat."

Frank and Luke dug into the soft, juicy fruit while Bill watched, occasionally helping himself to a scoop when his friends were busy chewing. It tasted like the jungle air on its very best day, wet and sweet, and it tickled his throat.

The three of them slumped against a cool, mossy stone and digested, juices running down their chins.

"Luke is just back from an adventure," said Bill. "Got trapped in quicksand and everything."

"Dang," said Frank. "Sounds dicey."

"It was pretty scary," Luke admitted. "But I was moving quickly and relied on my training."

"I saw a howler monkey stuck in that mess once," Frank said with a chuckle. "He was howlin' all right!"

"I'll bet," said Bill. Frank wasn't always the most sensitive creature, but as usual Bill brushed it off and changed the subject, blaming the Pet's youth and awkwardness. "What does Pablo have you doing today?"

"All sorts of junk," said Frank. "I was guardin' the perimeter . . ."

"That's the job you get when they just want you out of their feathers," Bill explained to Luke.

"Hey, works fine for me," said Frank. "I was just chillin' in the brush, mindin' my own. Even saw myself a bona fide Jungle Eagle."

"Are you kidding me?" Bill asked.

The eagle was one of the jungle's rarest and most

elusive species. They glided high in the sky, presiding over the forest. They were spotted only occasionally, when they swooped down to snack on animals as large as armadillos. Despite their fierce reputation, Bill saw them as an inspiring mix of grace and power, and he had often said that if he hadn't been born a Teddycat, he'd have liked to be an eagle.

"One hundred percent I am not kiddin'," said Frank. "Thing had talons the size of antlers."

"You saw a Jungle Eagle?" Luke asked, eyebrow arched. "Today?"

"Them talons were a mess, too," said Frank. "Must have just ripped somethin' up. Ouch!"

Luke was steaming mad. "Buddy, I just got back from a long cut through the jungle . . ."

"I think we've covered this?" said Bill.

"And if you've really been out there in the wild," Luke continued, "you'll know that the Jungle Eagle has hauled out of this whole valley, part of the rainy season migration."

"You sure about that?" Bill asked.

"Sure am," said Luke, leveling a quizzical glare at Frank. "In fact, they're usually the first to leave, while some other species drag their feet."

"So what do you say, Frank?" asked Bill. "Are you sure it was a Jungle Eagle?"

Frank, with his signature stammering chuckle, brushed off the question. "Who knows? I'm all jacked up on jackfruit, buddy. What do you want from me?"

"I want the truth!" said Luke. "See, this is what I mean when I say there's something strange going on here."

"Slow down," said Bill. "I'm sure it's an honest mistake."

"Deny it all you want, Bill, but I know you know what I'm talking about."

"Y'all are crazy," said Frank. "I'm gettin' out of here."

"Everybody relax!" cried Bill. "So Frank saw an eagle. So what?"

"Yeah!" said Frank. "So what!"

"So what?" said Luke. "So *what*? So I just double-timed my way across the jungle, trying to convince my family to follow me back here. And that was *your* idea, Bill! I vouched for you, for the Teddycats, and for Horizon Cove, and you *still* won't take me seriously when I say something funky is going down."

"Funky?" said Frank. "Sounds good to me."

Bill tried to hush Frank's running commentary and address Luke's concerns, but the Olingo wasn't out of steam just yet.

"And guess what?" said Luke. "I don't feel safe here anymore, so see ya around—I'm headin' back to the Olingo den! And if you're smart, you'll follow."

Luke stormed off, generating significant guff from his small body.

"Don't do that, Luke," Bill shouted after him. "Come on."

But Luke didn't slow down and Bill didn't follow, and eventually the Olingo disappeared into a blinding shaft of sunlight. Bill was struck with immediate pangs of regret. It seemed no matter how hard he tried to nurture Luke's friendship and value his company, he found a way to drive him away. But Bill refused to share Luke's misgivings. This was Horizon Cove, the Teddycats' destiny. They had already lost so much, Bill couldn't bear the thought of losing Horizon Cove too.

He turned to Frank and sighed. "Sorry about that."

"Good riddance, I say!" hollered Frank. "Never liked me an Olingo. Rude as rhinos."

Bill flinched and felt the heat gather in his snout. No matter how frustrated he might be with Luke, he didn't take kindly to the rehashing of old jungle stereotypes. Obviously the Olingos had a bad rep—even Bill would agree that rhinos were generally boorish—but the idea behind inviting them to Horizon Cove had been to move beyond all that.

Not to mention, Luke had saved Bill's life and was an honorary Teddycat. Frank had made him laugh, but Bill still didn't know what the Pets were, or what they were planning.

Chapter 20

THE GUSHING WATER was so loud it woke Bill from a nightmare. He struggled to drag himself to the opening of his den, eyes still screwed tight with sleep. Others were racing down to the water, which splashed against Polly's recent fortifications.

Ironically, Bill's nightmare had taken place in a desert, with no water in sight, a place so inhospitable that every species—the Pets, the Teddycats, even the humans—appeared as thin and spotty as a mirage. But beyond their shaky images, the Pets had been aggressive and quarrelsome, eyes narrowing against their beaks, feathers sharpened and almost glowing with fury.

Bill shook his head but his mind remained in the desert, stuck in the nightmare, his mouth dry as sand. In the clearing, Pets and Teddycats jostled over access to the overflow, wading into the muck and plucking swollen worms and grubs out of the ground, and Bill was hit with a realization like a tidal wave: This was the second sign!

The water announced the imminent arrival of the rainy season. It gathered in the mountains and cut its way down to the valley, building in volume and force. First came the wind, which swept the clouds into place, and then came the groundwater, forcing everything to the surface.

On cue, the worms popped like buds, sprouting in the grass amid the clearing's signature flowers. And the flood brought other changes: The clearing grew misty as the sun fired it to a crystalline brightness; rainbows formed, reaching into the shady underbrush. The Teddycats chased these figments, swatting at the colors with their paws as the Pets gleefully plucked worms from the soggy earth with a practiced slurp of the beak. Their knobby frames began to streamline, and their feathers were brighter than ever, bristling with an unnerving energy.

Bill felt sick to his stomach. He dug through a pile of his belongings in the den and found the feather Raffi the tapir had given him. The feather was multicolored and reflective, and it matched the frightening appearance of the Pets in his dream. He instinctively sniffed the feather, and the musty rot that still clung to it shot through his snout and watered his eyes. He threw it to the ground like a dart, where it stuck. There was no doubt in Bill's mind: It was a Pet feather.

Just what had Raffi been trying to tell him? Bill turned his eyes from the clearing as the Pets gorged themselves on the swollen worms, and the Teddycats frolicked in the freshly formed pond. He peered through the nest's woven walls at the distant peak where he had met the strange animal.

A voice pulled him back: "This is getting out of control."

It was Maia, arms crossed in the den's entrance. Behind her, other Teddycats edged slowly through the clearing, disturbed by the feeding Pets' bloodthirsty gusto.

"I've never felt so bad for a worm before," said Bill.

"Am I crazy?" Maia asked. "This is the second sign before the rain, right?"

"As far as I know," said Bill.

"What are they still *doing* here?" Maia muttered.

"I've tried to be patient," said Bill. "I mean, we know

how hard it is to leave a place you love, right?"

"Well, sure," said Maia. "But is that what this is?"

"I don't know *what* this is," said Bill. "And I don't know how to bring up the subject without appearing ungrateful. I mean, they saved our lives."

"Maybe there's another way to ask," said Maia.

She wore a thoughtful frown. Bill was impressed with her ability to stay cool, no matter the situation. Even during their worst moments together—Elena's kidnapping, Bill's banishment, Maia's run-in with snapping crocs—she managed to stay cool and collected. Bill had never doubted her strength or determination. Maia was a dedicated older sister to Elena and a bold and daring Teddycat warrior. She had encouraged Bill's rescue mission and helped to lead the escape from Cloud Kingdom as the humans attacked. She was wise, and she would never ask another Teddycat to do something that she wouldn't.

Bill's heart warmed with hope as he realized the extent of his confidence in her abilities. He knew from his mother that an important part of leadership was listening, knowing whom to trust, and letting those best suited take the reins. Well, Bill had spent his entire time in the Nest trying to figure out what Pablo and the Pets were thinking, with nothing to show for it.

If Maia had a better way, it was past time they tried it.

PABLO'S BEAK WAS smeared with worm guts. He nodded as Bill talked, though it was clear his attention was elsewhere.

"You know Maia, right?" asked Bill.

"Of course," said Pablo, swallowing. Bill and Maia looked away as the lump struggled down the Pet's gullet. Up close, the Pets, for all their industry and cleverness, were almost repulsive. Their bodies radiated unpleasantness in ways that attracted, and then repelled, the senses. Their colors drew the eye, only to blind and confuse. Their scent was a powerful defense on its own. Even the shapes of their bodies, the very systems that kept them alive, were arranged in a way that prompted other creatures to leave them be. Of course, everybody in the jungle was equipped with something. The Teddy-cats had their claws, frogs had their poisons, turtles had their shells. But it was still startling to see a fellow forest resident deploy its powers even after a peaceful relationship had been established. The Pets' inability to turn off their defenses almost made Bill feel sorry for them.

"Look," said Maia, once Pablo had worked the worms down to his gut, "we're just worried about you guys. I mean, shouldn't you leave before it's too late? The rains will be here any day!"

Pablo laughed. "That's not your concern."

"What do you mean?" pressed Bill. "We live here, too. We have a right to know what's causing this delay. What will the rains bring? What happens if you're still here when they come?"

"Is there not plenty for you to eat? Plenty to drink? Aren't you safe and warm in your dens, our nests? Aren't you still alive and breathing after your encounter with the crocs? These are your concerns. As I said on your first day here, 'Hold all questions until the end.'"

The Pet's eyes swelled with hunger and glee. He shot his head down to the grass and sucked a worm up from the mud. It made a loud, slurping sound. Bill and Maia couldn't help but turn away, their snouts wrinkled in disgust.

"WELL, THAT DIDN'T work," said Maia, trudging back toward the Garra den. "Sorry. Thought that might open up the lines of communication, but that big bird won't budge."

"Are you kidding?" said Bill. "We learned a ton."

"Oh yeah?" said Maia. "Like what?"

"Like . . ." Bill thought for a second. "Plug your ears with grass before attending WormFest."

Maia laughed. "Yes. Avoid direct eye contact with a worm-eating Pet."

They commiserated together, laughing at their own discomfort. Bill climbed up into the den and turned to help Maia. They flopped over onto the floor and rolled to a halt.

"We did learn some things, though," said Bill. "We pushed Pablo, and he pushed back. That tells me there's something he doesn't want us to know. Besides, I have another idea. A weird little guy gave me this feather a while back. What do you think?"

Bill pulled the feather from the den floor and handed it over to Maia. She reached for it, then suddenly drew back her paw.

"Ouch!" she cried.

"What happened?"

"It cut me!" Maia yelped, sucking on the wound.

Bill peered closely—the feather had indeed sliced her paw, clean and deep. "We need to dress that. Where's my mother? Have you seen her?"

They needed Marisol's hospital experience, and

soon. Maia's paw was seeping blood, and the color had already drained from her face.

"No problem," said Bill. "We'll get you fixed up."

"I'm feeling a little . . . woozy," said Maia.

"Let's get you settled down here," said Bill. He made sure her head was propped up against the den wall so she would stay upright and awake. Maia's fur was slick and dark with blood. Bill felt dizzy just from the sight of it. But at his core he remained sure of Maia's well-being: She had stared down tougher foes than a cut to the paw.

"Rest here. I'll be right back," said Bill.

"Stay with me," Maia pleaded. "I don't want to be here alone."

"You won't be alone!" said Bill. "How could you think that? My mother is just outside. I'll be back in a jiffy. Everything will be fine."

"Promise?" asked Maia, her eyelids heavy.

"I promise," said Bill, and he knew that she believed him.

MARISOL AND BIG Bill were surveying the hubbub developing around the pond in the low end of the clearing.

Teddycats and Pets were still tearing at the ground, hunting and collecting worms. Bill had to give Polly credit—her fortifications were solid. The rush could have ripped through the clearing, cutting Horizon Cove in two as it made its way down to the hunting grounds and the river, but instead it was trapped, dammed by Polly for use in the Nest. Used thoughtfully, the water could last the Teddycats for the whole year and keep the garden happy and healthy. For now, it was a glorified soaking pool. There had been a spring back in Cloud Kingdom that the Elders had frequented, claiming it had restorative powers. And just like old times, there was Finn, floating with his eyes closed and a dreamy expression on his face.

"He seems to be enjoying himself," muttered Big Bill. "Takin' a swim in our water reserves."

Bill raced to his parents and wrapped both arms around Marisol. "Mom, I need your help. Maia's hurt."

"What happened?" asked Marisol, eyes wide as she crouched to meet her son.

"She cut her hand," said Bill. "She's bleeding a lot."

Marisol's face settled into a look of grim determination. "Take me to her."

In the den, Maia was still awake, but her head drooped and her eyes were distant. Marisol got straight to work, preparing a wrap with a mixture of berries, roots, and flowers. Bill knew from experience that the medicine stung something awful—but it also worked.

"Here we go, honey," said Marisol, kneeling before her patient.

She lifted Maia's limp arm and examined the wounded paw. Maia yelped as Marisol applied the wrap to the cut, but the bleeding stopped almost immediately.

"Bill, get some water, please," said Marisol, polite yet firm.

Well, it's the right day for that, thought Bill, ripping out of the den and down to the nearest puddle. In frantic motions he cupped as much water as he could and rushed it back to his mother.

"Hold it to her mouth," Marisol counseled. "That's it."

Maia lapped at the water in Bill's palms, and slowly the color began to return to her features.

"Thank you, Bill," said Marisol, as she smoothed Maia's fur with calming strokes.

"That was scary," said Bill.

"What happened?"

"I was just showing . . ."

"It was my fault," croaked Maia, glaring at Bill. "I tripped and fell."

"Poor thing," said Marisol. "You'll be better in no time. Lie and rest as long as you'd like."

"Thanks, Mrs. Garra, but I have to get back to my den," said Maia. She pulled herself up and limped toward the exit.

"I'll walk her home," said Bill, shouldering some of Maia's weight.

"That's sweet," said Marisol. "Let me know if you need anything else."

"Thanks, Mrs. Garra," said Maia. "You really saved the day."

"We'll see," said Marisol, as the Pets chomped away in the background.

"WHY DID YOU lie to my mom?" Bill asked as they made their way back to Maia's den.

"It wasn't really a lie," said Maia. "I just don't think we should tell anyone about that feather until we know what we're dealing with."

"What do you mean?"

Maia grunted in frustration. "The Pets aren't going anywhere, and now we find out that their feathers can change colors and are sharp to the touch? How strange do these birds need to be before we decide to take them seriously?"

"You really think . . ."

"Look, Bill, I know you want Horizon Cove to be great," said Maia. "So do I. Really. And it *can* be great, but right now it has some serious problems. Are you willing to face them?"

"What should I do?" Bill asked quietly.

"You have to find whoever gave you that feather."

Chapter

21

PROPELLED BY MAIA'S wise words, Bill returned to the waterfall where he had last seen Raffi. It was easier to follow the creek bed now that it was swollen with mountain runoff. The sound of the waterfall was like thunder. It filled Bill's head and made the ground shake. It was a force, just like the current itself.

Bill climbed the rock face with a renewed vigor, inspired by the friends who'd been hurt: Maia, Luke, Omar, Elena, Diego. If he had placed them in danger by following the Pets, then he had to make that right. Even amid the chaos of the jungle, this quick succession of near-deadly accidents was unusual and worth examining further. Bill just hoped that he could finally see them for what they were. He wasn't exactly sure how Raffi could help, but the little calf was the only creature so far that had anything to say about the Pets. Well, he hadn't really *said* anything, but the feather had to mean something.

But when Bill pulled himself onto the grassy mesa, he saw no sign of Raffi. It was disappointing, but he knew that in the jungle everything was always in flux, and nobody stayed in one place. Bill consoled himself with the mesa's majestic view, which rolled down to the hunting ground and beyond. Behind him, the jungle continued its upward climb, toward the upper reaches of the same volcanic peaks that had given rise to Cloud Kingdom.

The air felt similar, thin but clean. Bill took a few deep breaths in the relative peace. The waterfall was still loud, but the steep rock and the heady altitude dimmed it to a mere rumble. Bill closed his eyes and tried to focus on the rumble, on the water, and let his mind go clear. He was grateful to Maia for the kick in the pants, but he also felt that he had somehow drifted away from the Teddycat who had led his species through the jungle, following an almost divine hunch. These days, none of Bill's hunches felt divine. Instead they felt muddy and slippery.

Bill opened his eyes and spotted a figure in the near distance. His heart leapt—perhaps it was Raffi! He almost let out a cry, before remembering himself. In the jungle it was best to identify somebody before alerting them to your existence. Shouting with unabashed glee was an old Cloud Kingdom habit, and one that could get you killed in the wilder stretches of the jungle.

Slowly, the figures came into focus. It wasn't Raffi at all, but Omar and one of the Pets!

Omar seemed somehow smaller than the last time Bill saw him. It had been a while, longer than Bill realized. He had simply pushed Omar out of his mind after their last ugly parting. And the Pet with him was an especially strange one, dragging alongside Omar with a crooked gait, tufts of missing feathers, and red eyes.

Distress ran down Bill's spine. Omar appeared healthy and normal, but what was he doing so far from the Nest? And who was this Pet? Questions piled up in Bill's head until the calm he had so recently achieved was crowded out.

"Hey, Omar," he said, somewhat carefully. "What brings you out here?"

"Hello," said Omar. Up close his eyes held a vacant expression, as if Bill were a stranger, and his voice was soft and flat.

"I haven't seen you since my walk with Maia," Bill continued. "I'm sorry about that, by the way. I didn't mean those things I said. Well, I meant some of them, but we've been through so much together, an occasional argument is no big thing, right?"

"Hello," Omar said again, that one word stumbling out of his mouth. The Pet stood close behind, and Bill could smell its sour funk.

"Yes," said Bill. "*Hello*. Who's your friend here?"

He had expected the run-in to be awkward, given their last meeting, but this was something else, something seeming more malicious.

"Drago," said the Pet, in an apparent introduction.

"That's it?" said Bill, laughing. "Nice to meet you, Drago."

Again, silence, nothing but the Pet's stink.

"O, it's me!" shouted Bill, waving his paws. But Omar's eyes were unfocused and refused to meet Bill's pleas.

"Is this about Maia?" Bill asked. "Because you *know* she wants us to be friends again."

Omar and the Pet drifted off, the Pet stumbling as Omar moved slowly and seemingly without direction. Bill scratched his head as he watched them go.

"See you back at the Nest," Bill said warily. He didn't know if he had lost Omar as a friend or whether a fellow Teddycat was in trouble. He needed to get back to the

Nest and figure it all out. Bill took one last look around for Raffi, hoping he might be hiding or sleeping in the grass, but the tranquility of the mesa had been pierced by the passage of Omar and that dingy Pet, and a chill in Bill's chest convinced him nothing good would come from staying.

INSTEAD OF CLIMBING back down the bluff, Bill decided to take the long way home. He retreated into the forest at the other end of the ledge and sloped down in a lazy arc. The vegetation was dense, but the slope allowed for a natural momentum, and Bill let himself go until he was nearly sledding down the slanted forest floor.

There were no vines to grab and swing, just exposed networks of smooth roots stretched across jagged rocks slick with moss and obscured by heavy curtains of mist. When he was on the verge of losing control, Bill slowed himself with his claws, digging into the ground or passing trees. The blast of the waterfall—now hidden from view—was ominous. It could have been a monster bellowing in a cave or some crack in the earth.

Just as the ground began to level, a small glade appeared, dug into a notch in the mountainside. Bill skidded to a stop and took a moment to collect himself. Swaths of mist rolled past, lapping at his fur. His vision was slightly shaky, from both the exertion and the uneven terrain, and his lungs burned as he filled them again and again. It felt good.

Rock jutted over the glade, sheltering it. From the top, thick vines and thorny weeds shot down, forming something like a trap that resembled the shroud the Pets had thrown over the Nest when there had been rumors of Joe headed their way. But the glade was so wild, and so far from the clearing, that Bill didn't know what could possibly be hiding behind the vines. Still, he thought he spotted some movement and drew closer, peering between them.

Bill gasped. It was filled with crocs, a whole line of them. Drips of water fell from the dark rock and landed on their scales. But the crocs didn't gnash their teeth, leap, or chomp. Instead they just lay there, sullen and forlorn. The evil glow Bill recalled from their last attack seemed to have left their eyes, and all that remained was a vacancy that felt eerily familiar.

Once the shock wore off, Bill clapped his paws together a few times in an attempt to get a rise out of the crocs. If just one of them snarled or lunged, Bill could leave the glade satisfied. But all the crocs could do was moan, haunting croaks that rumbled up through their long bellies.

"Not so tough now, are ya?" said Bill, though with the crocs penned up the taunt felt a bit forced and undeserved.

Bill remembered what it had been like locked inside the humans' cage, when he didn't know if he would ever see his family or friends again. He wouldn't wish that pain on just anybody, but the crocs had presented themselves as open enemies of the Teddycats, and Bill felt safer knowing they weren't roaming free. But who had conquered the crocs and broken their spirit in such spectacular fashion? It had to be the humans, thought Bill. He shuddered as he considered the possibilities of a croc and human alliance. He would have to report the finding to his father and Pablo. If Joe was locking away crocs, Teddycats and Pets wouldn't be far behind.

"Oh, quit your bellyaching," said Bill as the crocs continued to moan, but they stared right past him. A nearby rustle sent Bill scurrying up the closest tree, a stubby, overgrown bush. He burrowed into its foliage as the rustle grew louder.

A Pet entered the glade, and the crocs began to moan once more. Bill didn't recognize the Pet, but just as he was about to hop out of hiding and warn it about the crocs, the Pet began to stuff bunches of flowers through the vines. He definitely recognized the flowers—the entire clearing was filled with them. While Bill didn't enjoy their flavor—the petals held a gritty sweetness that made his gums itch—the rest of the Teddycats had been devouring them paw over fist ever since they first arrived at the Cove.

Bill's mind spun as the Pet continued to feed its prisoners and encourage them to eat the flowers piling up before them. Did the Pets control the crocs in some way, beyond just captivity? They were oddly docile as they accepted the flowers from the Pets, even cooperative. Bill had never seen anything like it. All the crocs he'd ever encountered had been wily and ruthless. He wondered whether these crocs were prisoners or weapons, agents under Pet control. And what did this mean for the Teddycats?

The Pet acting as warden was as stiff and graceless as the rest of them, but hulking. Suddenly it turned around—it was Polly! Bill sunk further into the brush and decided not to make his presence known, and as she stalked about the glade, Bill quietly scampered away, back down the mountainside.

Chapter

22

BY THE TIME Bill arrived at the Nest it was dinnertime. While his mind was still brimming with questions, it was clear that the Pets were extraordinary creatures, able to capture one of the jungle's fiercest predators. Their mastery of the crocs, along with their battle prowess and den-camouflaging skills, proved their ability to survive in the jungle despite severe physical challenges. Bill hoped the Pets would pass on their tricks to the Teddy-cats before leaving for the rainy season. He wouldn't mind teaching those crocs a lesson.

Bill's stomach growled as he approached the Garra den. He followed his father's snores, which could be heard from all the way across the clearing. Bill lingered for a moment outside, amid the flowers and beneath the ongoing construction of the Teddycats' new dwelling. The moon was wide, almost pulsing, and it lit the Nest with an eerie glow.

But inside the den it was warm and dry as Marisol prepared dinner and Big Bill snoozed in the corner. "And where have you been?" whispered Marisol.

Bill had always found it funny that his mother tiptoed around her sleeping husband while he produced noises that could wake up a hibernating snake pit.

"Just looking for something," said Bill.

Marisol shushed him, eyes leaping to Big Bill's rising and falling chest.

"I know," said Bill. "I see him. What's for dinner? I'm starved."

"Another Nest specialty," said Marisol, assembling whatever grasses, slugs, flowers, and flesh the Pets had provided. While some of the Teddycats continued to refuse the meat, others—like the Garras—searched for ways to blend it into their diets.

"I don't think we should eat those flowers anymore," said Bill.

"Why not?" Marisol asked, absentmindedly plucking a few from the pile.

Bill felt his heart swell. He had to tell them what he

had seen in the forest—Omar and Drago, the crocs and Polly—but he didn't know where to begin. A lump rose in his throat.

"Yes, why not?"

Bill turned. It was Pablo, neck craned through the den entrance.

"Oh, Pablo, you're right on time," said Marisol. "I was just about to wake Mr. Garra."

"Don't rush on my account," said Pablo. "I want to hear Bill's concerns."

"Maybe you should start," said Marisol. "I don't want Bill to be confused."

"What's going on?" Bill asked.

"Nothing," said Marisol. "Pablo just told your father and me that you might have seen something a bit . . . troubling today, and he wanted to talk with you, just so you won't be frightened or confused."

"I don't know what you're talking about," said Bill, careful not to give too much away.

"There's nothing to be afraid of," said Pablo. "I just want to get a few things straight."

"I'm all ears," said Bill.

Marisol nudged Big Bill, who rose with a grumble.

"Pablo, welcome," said Big Bill. "And Bill, we're glad to see you've made it home."

"I wasn't gone that long," said Bill.

It seemed to Bill that ever since the Teddycats had arrived at Horizon Cove, his whereabouts had been closely followed. At first he had suspected the Elders of watching him, but now he wasn't so sure. Was it actually the Pets on his tail?

"Regardless," said Big Bill, "let's hear what Pablo has to say."

"And dinner?" Bill asked. The lump was gone, but his stomach was really howling, and he felt slightly faint.

"After!" boomed Big Bill.

"Yes, sir," said Bill, startled by his father's reaction.

Pablo cleared his throat. "We know you saw the crocs, Bill. But don't worry—you're not in trouble. In fact, this was one of the harder things for us to share, and it's one of the reasons we haven't left yet despite the impending rains."

"I'm listening," said Bill.

"We're glad you stumbled on that cage," said Pablo. "You're a smart little Teddycat. I know the Nest, and all of Horizon Cove, will be safe with you."

Despite Bill's misgivings, he couldn't help but take pleasure from these words. Still, the imprisoned crocs with their vacant stares were burned into his memory.

"But how are you controlling them?"

"Predators are the jungle's number one threat," said Pablo. "You must know that by now. If not for the humans, Cloud Kingdom would still be the sanctuary you once knew. Over the years, we Pets have learned ways to control some of these predators. We have outsmarted them, trapped them, just like the humans do. But unlike the humans, we do not kill them. Instead, we hold them captive until they see that we're not worth pursuing. We try to steer them toward a better way, one in which we all coexist in peace. So far we've had very encouraging results, and I expect the crocs to be set free any day now."

This was a lot for Bill to process. While it was certainly good news that the crocs might no longer pose a threat, Bill was still wary of the Pets' methods. Where did their powers end?

"We take care of them," continued Pablo. "You saw Polly feeding the crocs. It's a good system. Once the process is complete and they are ready to be released, I don't expect to have an issue with the crocs ever again."

Bill looked over at his parents, who seemed impressed.

"Crocs at your beck and call?" said Big Bill. "Now that's really something."

"I treated many croc wounds in Cloud Kingdom," said Marisol. "They were truly ghastly. It sure would be nice not to have to fear those creatures anymore."

"Well, hopefully the threat of crocs will soon be a thing of the past," said Pablo. "The jungle is always moving forward—isn't that right, Bill?"

"That's true," said Bill. It was something he had learned the hard way, and it was a lesson underlined by the sacrifices of Felix and all the others the Teddycats had lost along the way. But the sentiment somehow felt different coming from Pablo.

"With that all finished, let's eat!" said Marisol.

"Unfortunately, I must decline," said Pablo. "See you all in the morning?"

"Of course," said Marisol. "Bill, would you like to begin?"

"Actually, I'm not really that hungry anymore," said Bill. His gut felt squeezed and flattened as Pablo took his leave.

"Suit yourself," said Big Bill. "More for me."

SLIVERS OF MOONLIGHT slanted through cracks in the den walls, but Bill couldn't sleep. Though a cloak of darkness had fallen, Bill couldn't help but think about his time in the Nest and all the ways things had changed since the Teddycats arrived. Something was amiss. By neglecting their migration and imprisoning predators, the Pets were demonstrating a willingness to disrupt the rhythm of the jungle. While these changes might serve the Pets well, Bill knew every species would feel the disturbance.

As Bill knew all too well, no action was without its consequences, and no deed—even one with good intent—went unpunished. That meant the Pets had calculated the damage wrought by a late start against . . . well, that was the thing: Bill didn't know the other half of the calculation just yet. He needed to talk to Maia. She deserved to know about Omar, about the crocs, and about Pablo's claims. Maia had a brilliant way of breaking down information—she could cut right through the millions of scenarios that Bill might concoct and focus on the real issues, or at least the most plausible possibilities. She was a listener *and* a fighter, and he needed both now more than ever.

Bill's restlessness made the night feel especially long and lonely . He peered through one of the wider slats in the den and idly watched the moon splash against the clearing. He blinked at the sight of movement, a slight fold in the calm grass.

Bill narrowed his eyes. There it was again! Suddenly the moon dialed in like a spotlight, exposing Raffi's small, shiny form.

"Hey, Raffi!" Bill huffed through the den's woven wall. "Over here!"

The tapir placed a finger to his stubby snout, and Bill hushed, waiting as Raffi waddled closer to the Garra den. Soon they were a mere foot apart. It was strange to see Raffi in the clearing—Bill associated him with the wilds of the cliff and the roar of the waterfall—but the tapir appeared to be at peace in the wider world, a true citizen of the jungle, carrying himself with an uncanny confidence that Bill was sure could ward off most any threat.

Raffi, still signaling for silence, rolled his big eyes up, toward the canopy.

"What is it?" Bill asked. His parents were still asleep beside him, and he didn't want to wake them by sneaking out of the den. "What are you trying to tell me?"

Raffi pulled his hoof away from his snout and pointed it toward the sky. Bill followed suit, but all he saw were trees, the canopy where the Teddycats would one day live. Construction had continued after the Diego and Elena debacle, though Bill had made himself scarce. The project hung unfinished between the branches, vines holding the planks in place.

A bolt struck Bill and flashed through his body. His fur stood straight and his claws curled. He closed his eyes and saw the Teddycats squeezed into these tiny gaps in the canopy, hidden away from the jungle floor and as isolated and contained as any floppy croc. Raffi giggled as Bill struggled to speak.

"That's it!" Bill cried at last. "The new den!"

Chapter

23

DAWN CAME QUICKLY, and as soon as it did Bill burst forth into the clearing, searching for Maia. He knew Polly had assigned the Teddycats various jobs, but he didn't want to ask her for Maia's location and risk a confrontation about the crocs. So, he ducked behind a stone when he saw her picking flowers by the garden. She looked different to him now—stranger and more powerful—though he didn't know if she actually had the ability to control the crocs or if she was only in charge of feeding them. Either way, he didn't want to take any chances. He would find Maia on his own.

Bill took to the trees, determined to rifle through the canopy until he found his confidante. He had so many things to tell her, he didn't even know where to start. Omar's behavior and Drago's hulking menace didn't make sense without the imprisoned crocs, and the fact that his new hunch concerning the den came from a mysterious tapir left Bill with some lingering questions of credibility.

Then Bill remembered the feather—he would lead with the feather and its deep cut. The feather connected the Pets to Raffi, and Raffi to Maia. Everything else he would have to explain to her as best he could.

He zipped past other groups of Teddycats working diligently on the new den until at last he spotted Maia. She was simply rigging vines into a web, but Bill's fresh suspicions cast a sinister application on all the tasks assigned to the Teddycats. Those vines could easily become chains.

Bill called Maia's name as he approached. The last thing he wanted was to startle her. She looked up from her work and smiled. "Hello!" she said.

Bill's heart sank. He wished he had good news to share.

Maia could see the sullen look on Bill's face. "Just tell me," she said. "Just let it out."

These had been her words when he had to break the news of Elena's disappearance. Even if they didn't exactly give him strength, they gave him no choice but to pursue the truth.

The truth: That's what Maia, and all the Teddycats, deserved, and Bill wouldn't stop until it was uncovered.

He took a deep breath.

ONCE BILL FINALLY finished talking, Maia burst out into laughter. "The Pets are helping us," she said. "We need to be grateful. Without them, who knows what might have happened to us?"

"That's exactly what I used to think," said Bill. "But we were right to be suspicious. First off, quit working on this stupid den—it's a trap!"

"How is it a trap?" Maia asked, still tying the vines.

"They're going to keep us locked away up here," said Bill. "Just like the crocs."

"It'll be a safe, secure structure high in the trees, just like we always wanted."

"That's not what we wanted," Bill insisted. "Remember? We wanted to be one with the jungle. We wanted to become citizens, carve a life out of the wild, not run and hide back in the trees. They're using our fears against us. This isn't the vision that led us to Horizon Cove—it's just

Cloud Kingdom all over again, except the Elders have been replaced by Pets, and it's not even really our home. Do you really want to feel like a captive for the rest of your life?"

"You aren't making sense," said Maia.

"*You* aren't making sense," cried Bill. "Everything we talked about: the rains, the feather that cut your paw. You were suspicious too! Have you just forgotten everything?"

"Look," said Maia, finally dropping the vine's knot into her lap. "I know what you saw was scary. It would freak me out too. But there's a perfectly good explanation. The Pets—"

"How do you know what I saw?" asked Bill.

Maia shrugged, then returned to her task. "Pablo mentioned you might come see me about this."

"Don't you think that's strange?" asked Bill. "Why is Pablo tracking me everywhere I go? Why is he telling *you* about it?"

"You're a popular guy," said Maia, shrugging.

Bill shook his head. "Maia, this isn't you. The real you would take this seriously."

He looked deep into her eyes, searching for the vacant, glazed expression he had found in Omar and the crocs, but there was only Maia's usual poise. Yet while her eyes were the same, her courage and kindness were gone, and an icy wind rushed through the trees as Bill's friend coldly dismissed him.

"Just leave me alone," Maia sneered.

Chapter

BILL SLID DOWN the trunk like it was a pole. He decided to tell everybody. There had to be somebody left to believe him!

The sounds of the Teddycats working on the den infuriated him—every cut, every tree, every vine was another chain they'd need to break to be free from the Pets. His heart ached from Maia's dismissal, but he had decided that it was not her fault: Something was affecting the minds of the Teddycats he loved, and he was determined to get them back to the way they were. He grieved for Maia but took solace in the fact that even the Pets couldn't fully squash her verve. And even if he didn't always get along with Omar, he'd take their prickly rapport over whatever the Pets had introduced.

The world sped by as Bill continued to drop from the canopy. He tried to ignore the Teddycats in the trees, blithely chopping away, using their claws against themselves. As Bill hit the ground with an unexpected thud, he vowed to never again do the dirty work of another species.

As Bill shook off the hard landing, he noted the looming Pets as they circled around him. Pablo's wings were spread, and the force of their stench walloped Bill's snout and made his eyes water. The Pets were molting, casting off their feathers as an angry rash attacked their skin.

"Whew," snorted Bill. "This has gone on long enough. Maybe you guys should stick around for the rains, because—and I mean this with all due respect—you stink."

The Pets directed angry glares at Pablo, who was in the best position to hurt Bill.

"I mean, really badly," Bill continued. "You all might consider soaking for a while, get a deep cleanse, 'cause I don't believe this is gonna be a one-scrub stink."

"Are you finished?" Pablo asked.

"I'm just getting started," said Bill. The break in civility was invigorating. He had spent too much time trying to please the Pets, forgetting that the most important things were his family and friends. *They* were who Bill should have been protecting, not the feelings of devious strangers. "You think you can trap the Teddycats? Please."

"Who said anything about a trap?" asked Pablo. "These Teddycats are working of their own accord, on a project that will benefit them."

"I know what you're trying to do," Bill hissed. "You want to imprison us, just like the crocs. But the Teddycats will never fall for it."

"It's already happened," said Pablo. He laughed and the other Pets joined in, honking and squawking away. "And I want to thank you, Bill Garra, for leading your species right to us. Couldn't have planned it better myself."

"The Teddycats don't belong to the Pets," said Bill. "We are freeborn citizens of the jungle, and we will never surrender! Nobody will stop us from fulfilling our destiny—not the crocs, not Joe, and especially not any Pets. I've got bad news for you, Pablo: Horizon Cove belongs to the Teddycats and the Olingos."

BILL FLAILED AND fumed as the Pets tightened the circle around him. Suddenly, a jagged light cracked the dark clouds, followed by a deep, rolling rumble, like the sky was about to break open and release a flood.

It was the final sign: The rains were imminent.

Bill's eyes widened, and he searched for an escape as the Pets craned their necks. Above them, the clouds had grown darker and heavier, sagging with rain.

The wind picked up as Bill screamed for the Teddycats to flee the trees. His family and friends were dazed, distracted by the growling sky.

"It's a trap!" he cried, but his words were swept away.

Other creatures raced through the clearing, searching for high ground before the rains descended and swallowed them whole. Snakes and birds slithered and screeched, reacting to the light and sound, heading for the hills. Bill spotted a waddling family of wanderoos—they were the Jungle Eagle's primary prey, slow and juicy. If the wanderoos were still around, there was no way the eagles were. Luke was right: Frank had been lying.

Amid the thunder and commotion, Bill scratched and struggled himself free from the scrum of Pets.

The Pets were consumed, distracted by the noise, the light, the gathering storm clouds, whipped-up winds, and scurrying invaders. Bill juked to the tree line and threw Pablo off balance, then slithered through Sally's skinny legs and bolted off into the clearing.

Chapter

25

WITH NO DIRECTION and no way of knowing which Teddycats were brainwashed, Bill had to find someone else to trust. And he knew exactly who to track down: the Olingos! If Bill could band together with Luke and his family to save the Teddycats and Horizon Cove, the two species would be together again, and finally home.

The sky cracked and rumbled again. Bill glanced up at the encroaching darkness as he hustled through the traffic. All the activity was sure to rouse predators, and Bill figured he might even be safer in the jungle. The edge of the forest beckoned.

Bill spotted Diego leaning against a tree, watching the creatures react to the weather, and against his better judgment decided to ask him for help—the old scout would be harder than just about anybody to brainwash, and he wouldn't be able to hide it well if he had.

"Quite a scene, eh?" said Diego, smiling at the madness.

"It's nuts!" said Bill.

"Seems like the Pets' plan was pretty much a lie, mate," said Diego.

"Seems like," agreed Bill.

"So what's your plan now?"

Bill decided to risk it all and tell Diego everything.

DIEGO'S JAW WAS clenched, chin resting against his chest. Throughout Bill's tale, his snout fired off angry snorts.

"I truly believe the Olingos are our best chance against the Pets," concluded Bill.

"Got it," said Diego. "Let's go find the Olingos, then."

"Just like that?" asked Bill, unable to mask his surprise. "You're in?"

"I've been givin' these birds the side-eye for a while now," said Diego. "Don't figure they've ever been on the level."

"So then why did you help me with the new den? You were almost killed!"

"Wanted to support you, mate," Diego said. "Don't want to be one of those Elders too afraid of change to let any other voice be heard. But something's definitely wrong, so let's get workin' to fix it."

"That's what I'm *talking* about!" said Bill, thrusting a closed paw into the air. Chills ran up his spine, and his eyes watered with tears of gratitude. He had never questioned Diego's loyalty to the Teddycats, but he was still getting used to the idea of having the old scout in his corner. It felt something like a miracle.

"Don't worry," said Bill. "You're a long way off from being an Elder."

"Eh, these things sneak up on ya," said Diego.

The sky lit up with clashing fire bolts. As soon as they disappeared, the rumble rose again. It sounded like a mountain collapsing, sending an avalanche their way.

"We need to move," said Diego, as the first enormous drop of rain landed on Bill's head.

THE RAIN FELL hard and steady, splashing against the canopy, running down the trees. Leaves, fronds, vines, and blossoms of every stripe sagged and doubled over beneath the weight of the water. Bugs and birds struggled to stay afloat. Even the dragonflies were soggy and sluggish. The clouds were low and black, and the clearing seemed to be shrinking as the canopy descended and branches swayed from the force of the storm. Bill fought his way back toward his den but soon realized he was lost and disoriented, standing in the middle of a wasteland that barely resembled the Nest. The ground turned to muck, sliding and shifting as the rain pounded against it. The surrounding forest was nowhere to be seen. Instead, everywhere he turned stood thick, gnarled walls of vegetation, as if from out of nowhere.

Bill took a deep breath and reminded himself that this was just another of the Pets' tricks. They were altering the Nest the same way they had hidden from Joe—by springing booby traps and draping every surface and corner with a blur of green. It was an impressively effective system: Bill had no idea where his den was. And Diego, to whom he had been speaking just moments ago, was also nowhere to be seen, lost in the sudden flash of rain and mud.

Slowly, Bill's eyes began to adjust to the darkness. He spun about, searching for seams in the Pets' veil. Though they were still hidden from sight, he could hear the Pets' wheezy squawks and Frank's unmistakable chuckle. He followed the sounds and eventually slipped between two rippling cloaks of foliage. For a moment, a glimpse of reality shimmered—his parents' den was within shouting distance. Bill buckled down and charged toward it before the whole place evaporated, like a mirage.

BILL COULD HEAR his father before he could see him. Big Bill was shouting into the storm, challenging the elements as they cracked and boomed.

"Do your worst!" he cried. "You won't wash my home away. My son's out there, wet and cold, but if you think you've come close to breaking our spirit, I've got some bad news for ya . . ."

For Bill this was both reassuring and embarrassing. He was relieved that his father was apparently unaffected by the Pets' powers, and he appreciated his father's bluster and bravado, but he didn't want to attract their tormentors' attention.

Bill dragged himself toward his father as the rain

intensified and the clearing continued to shrink. "Dad, get inside!"

"Is that you, son?" cried Big Bill. "Keep fighting the storm—you can make it!"

"I'm on my way!" huffed Bill.

"Hurry!" shouted Big Bill, a fatherly command as loud as any thunder.

BILL AND HIS father shook themselves dry. Despite everything, Bill had to laugh; he had never seen his father's fur so fuzzy. Big Bill had always loomed large, but after a thorough soaking and violent shake, he nearly doubled in size, barely leaving room for Bill and Marisol. The den rattled in the wind, and leaks sprung with each new spurt and gust, but compared to the raging storm outside, it was downright cozy.

"The Pets are controlling the Nest and almost everybody in it," said Bill, still panting from his escape. "That's why nothing looks right. And the new den? It's a trap. The Pets have tricked us into building our own prison! We need to fight back."

Bill watched his parents absorb the news. They

did so thoughtfully and without panic. This calmed Bill somewhat. He figured their composure was a natural result of a life spent in the jungle. As Felix had once said, everything could change in an instant.

"It'll be a tough battle," said Big Bill. "This is their turf."

"But it used to be ours," said Marisol.

"Exactly," said Bill. "And it will be again. I'm going to find the Olingos, and together we will take back Horizon Cove."

"I like the sound of that," said Big Bill. "But how will you fight your way through?"

"I just have to rely on the jungle to be its fierce, unmanageable self," said Bill.

"Use the chaos to your advantage," Big Bill murmured, rubbing his chin.

"It all sounds very dangerous," said Marisol.

"And there's no guarantee the Olingos will agree to help us," said Bill. "Luke already asked them to join us once before. But now that we truly need them . . . well, I'm hoping they'll come around."

"It's about time we set things right with those wily little guys," said Big Bill. "The Elders poisoned the Teddy-cats against the Olingos, just to ease our own guilt over abandoning them for Cloud Kingdom."

"I know all about it," said Bill. "Luke is my best friend, and he's pretty resentful."

"We did 'em dirty, all right." Big Bill nodded. His eyes lit up. "Should I come with you?"

"No!" said Bill and Marisol together.

"We just got you back," said Marisol.

"And I need to do this on my own," said Bill. "I brought everyone here and told them to make nice with the Pets. Once the cracks in their story started to appear, I ignored them, and now my friends are in danger."

"Who do they have under their control?" Marisol asked quietly.

"I first noticed Omar," said Bill, counting off the victims. "Then the gang of crocs, and then Maia."

"Oh no," said Marisol. "Not Maia!"

"Poor dear," said Big Bill.

"She's going to be all right," said Bill, hoping he sounded more confident than he felt. "As long as I'm alive she'll never be a slave."

"You're doing a very brave thing, Bill," said Marisol. "In the jungle there are no guarantees."

Big Bill grasped his son by the shoulders. "If you defeat the Pets," he began, "Horizon Cove will be led by the Teddycats, and they will be led by you."

The Garras embraced as their nest continued to leak and shiver. They huddled together that way for the rest of the night, steeling themselves for the dire fight ahead.

Chapter

THE RAIN CONTINUED through dawn, the clouds dense and angry, as the Pets circled the dark sky like vultures. Bill had spent the night dissecting the clearing, considering all the ways the Pets might try to alter its shape. By the time he bid Big Bill and Marisol an emotional farewell and zipped into the jungle, he had established several possible escape routes. He felt the Olingos tug at his chest, the same way he had once been led to Horizon Cove, and vowed to skirt, skip, or smash any obstacle that stood in his way.

Bill used his claws as he made his way through the muck and sludge. Every tree, plant, and structure had been beaten down by the night's rainfall. Some were splintered, while others just drooped. He shook his head as he marveled at the extent of the damage—whoever assumed control of the Nest would have their work cut out for them.

He kept his eye on the edge of the clearing and chased after it. Aware of the Pets' abilities, Bill didn't allow himself to get thrown off by the unexpected. While landmarks were still out of place, Bill ignored them and followed his instincts.

As the clearing's grass turned to scrubs and undergrowth, Bill felt eyes on him. He turned just as Polly descended, talons first. Bill yelped and, spotting a hollow tree trunk, leapt into it. The trunk was dark and slimy, but when he slid out the other end he was a hundred feet inside the forest, far from Polly's reach. Bill caught his breath, puffing away alone in the jungle. He had never noticed the Pets' hooked talons before. Polly's were so sharp, they almost resembled Teddycat claws. His head throbbed with confusion and his belly was queasy with fear, but there was no time to rest.

Bill lit out through the wilderness, grappling as the valley slowly rose. He passed the enormous tree he had climbed with Maia the day of his awful fight with Omar. The hill steepened, and Bill kept scrambling. As soon as he reached the top he could climb to the canopy and start to swing, but until then he had to stick to the ground. He knew there was a notch near the point, a deep crack that he'd crossed on his first trip to Horizon Cove. Bill fought through stands of stiff bristles and hurdles of fallen branches, hoping every time that the obstacle would fall away and reveal the gap waiting for him on the other side.

It felt strange to be heading back toward Cloud Kingdom. He knew it no longer existed—at least, not in any recognizable form—and had no desire to visit. But still, he felt its pull. Maybe he always would. Bill's legs burned as he continued to climb uphill; he *had* to be making progress. The notch was close. Once he cleared that, the whole jungle would open its arms and carry him the rest of the way. He could almost feel the wind brushing his fur.

But as he broke through another thorny hedge, he slid to a stop. His stomach clenched, then climbed up his throat. Standing before him was the very same tree he had climbed with Maia. He had gone in a circle.

Bill collapsed, tears in his eyes. He was angry and ashamed, frightened and frustrated. He thought he had beaten the Pets at their own game. Instead he was lost and alone, his spirit of resistance all but crushed. He looked ahead, then behind. Besides the tree, nothing was familiar. There was no telling where the Pets had led him or what they planned to do to him. Bill had no idea how to proceed. His thoughts were scattered, chased away by a panic that shook his body.

Despite his vulnerable state, there was no sign of his captors. Bill sniffled and considered his options. Maybe if he climbed all the way to the top of the tree, he could spot a way out of the Pets' maze. He shrugged and wiped his eyes and snout with the back of his paw—despite the storm and the rain, it was worth a shot.

The tree's roots towered over Bill as he clawed his way to the base of the trunk. His vision was still blurry, but he felt better—stronger, more focused—as he climbed. Just as the full width and scope of the tree began to unfold in his eyes, he caught sight of a small figure. Bill squinted and drew closer, quicker and quicker until his heart began to soar: It was Raffi, resting at the foot of the tree, waiting for him.

"The feather you gave me," said Bill. "It cut my friend."

Raffi frowned in apology. He was so small, his stripes were barely the width of the tree bark behind him.

"That was a Pet's feather, right?"

Raffi nodded.

"I guess those things are pretty dangerous," said Bill.

He wished Raffi would say something. It was as if he was muzzled, robbed of his voice. But there remained a deep reserve of wisdom in the tapir's silences as well as a slight sense of melancholy.

Raffi nodded again. Bill balled his fists in frustration, growing dizzy and despondent. The tapir couldn't tell him anything. They were doomed. The Pets had played him perfectly. Lulled into believing he could outsmart their defenses, he willingly drove himself deeper into their snare.

The tapir pulled itself up and tottered toward the other side of the tree. Reluctantly, Bill followed. The curve of the trunk seemed to go on forever, and Bill grew dizzy. Just when he thought he might need to stop and lean against the tree until the world stopped spinning, Raffi shot off into a fold in the forest. Two pronounced roots formed a channel that eventually ran into a basin of flat rock.

"Where are we going?" Bill asked, staying close. While he didn't expect answers, he felt compelled to ask his guide questions, and once he started it was hard to stop. "I need to get to the Olingos. You know any Olingos? What about Pets? Where'd you find that feather, anyway?"

Nothing but predictable silence from Raffi as they descended into a rocky hollow.

The tapir was surprisingly graceful considering its tiny legs, stepping quickly from stone to stone, although as they reached the bottom Bill wondered how it could possibly climb back up without help. Once they reached bedrock Raffi motioned to the smooth stone that surrounded the mouth of a dark, narrow cave.

Bill stepped back. The wall was crowded with drawings, some etched into the surface, others scrawled with berry juice and blood. Bill studied the images, and his heart rose up into his throat as the cave's terrifying story began to unfold.

Chapter

A STICK-FIGURE HUMAN gripped a small bird by its neck. Once released, the bird grew in size and strangeness, developing bizarre features with unnatural speed. Gradually it swelled to the size of a Pet, all crooked and bloated, neck and legs painfully stretched. Beneath them lay docile gatherings of crocs, tapirs, even Olingos.

Bill traced the drawings with his paw. "I know the Pets can control other species and change the layout of the forest. I saw the crocs when I went to find you by the waterfall. Why were you all the way up there?"

Raffi pressed his side against the wall, then went sniffing around the cave entrance.

"Right," said Bill. "The drawings."

He studied them more closely, searching for clues. He noticed that certain features were highlighted. For example, the crocs' teeth were huge. Of course, croc teeth *were* huge, but these were massive, out of scale with the rest of the sketch. Meanwhile, the tapirs wore large smiles, and the Olingos all had weirdly distended bellies.

The rain began to fall once more, forming quick puddles. Depending on how deep the cave went, the hollow would soon fill, drowning anything that couldn't make the climb to the surface.

"We'd better hurry up," said Bill. "It's not safe in here."

Raffi nudged the drawings again, and Bill traced the human stick figure.

"So their power comes from the humans. But what do the Pets want from us?"

Bill thought about the humans and the Teddy-cats, Cloud Kingdom in ash and ruins. What had they wanted? The claw, of course. He followed the wall as the rain picked up force—the water already covered Raffi's hooves. Subsequent illustrations showed the Pets shaking off feathers as they grew wide smiles, long teeth, and big bellies, while beneath them the number of imprisoned creatures dwindled. In the final drawing, the Teddycats joined the tapirs, crocs, and Olingos as the Pet—stink lines wafting from its body—bore down on its prey with vicious, familiar-looking talons.

"They want our claws, don't they? The same way they wanted the crocs' teeth and the tapirs' trustworthy appearance. They will imprison us until they absorb what they think is our most prized trait. But I'll tell you something, Raffi—Teddycats aren't just fierce because of our claws."

Raffi stared at him gravely. The water was nearly to his snout.

"What did they want with the Olingos' stomach?"

Raffi rubbed his belly, then belched.

"I guess they do have that tough scavenger gut," murmured Bill. He felt wiped out, overwhelmed by the powers of his enemy. "How're we supposed to defend against that? We can't, that's how! We gotta get out of Horizon Cove."

The rainfall swelled in the hollow. Water had already filled the cave.

"Well, first things first; we have to get out of here."

Bill scooped Raffi up and dug his claws into the freshly slick rock. He turned to take one last look at the drawings before they were submerged. In the final design a Teddycat flew through the air, claw raised, ready to clash with a flock of Pets. It filled Bill with a mixture of pride and fear.

He gave Raffi a protective squeeze. "Let's go."

Bill talked to himself as they climbed out of the hollow, working his way through the problem before him. "So the humans cursed the Pets, and now they think they can just steal what other animals earned through lifetimes of survival? I don't think so. Not on my watch, Raffi. But I guess that's why they stink so bad, huh? Feathers and skin falling off while they sprout mutations."

Bill shivered in disgust. "Almost makes me feel sorry for the cruddy critters, you know?"

Raffi let out a yelp of protest.

"Don't worry," said Bill. "Not really. Not after what they've done. They change their victims, isn't that right? However they control them, it causes changes. They stole the crocs' fighting spirit. Maybe they stole your voice. Is that what happened?"

Raffi grunted.

"Well, we're gonna go steal it back," said Bill. "But first we have to warn everyone. No time for the Olingos. Gonna have to do this on our own."

They reached the tree roots and scrambled up to the trunk's high ground. All around them the rain fell in sheets as the sky clapped and burst purple with violent bolts of light.

Bill looked at Raffi. “Any idea how to get back to the Nest?”

The tapir shrugged, snout dripping rain. He had already told Bill everything he knew.

Chapter

28

THE TWO WANDERED in what Bill hoped was the direction of the Nest. Instead of heading back down the hill, he continued to climb, hoping this risky bet might unravel the Pets' snare. Sure enough, Bill eventually spotted what he hoped was the same hollow tree he had used to escape Polly's attacks. There was no doubt in his mind about one thing: Those had been Teddycat claws on her talons, a terrifying sight that would make their battle for freedom all the more difficult.

The most immediate challenge, however, was finding a way to alert the Teddycats without tipping off the Pets. To complicate things further, early victims already under control might not leave willingly. The rain blew from the side, stinging Bill's face as he scrunched his forehead and tried to hatch a plan. What would convince the Teddycats to follow him one more time?

The wind carried a shriek through the storm-dark jungle. Bill's ears perked—it sounded like the cry of a Teddycat! He chased the sound as far as he could, until its echoes finally died down.

Bill waited, ready to pounce. The Teddycats were close—he could feel it.

Another shriek, closer. It almost sounded like they were calling his name.

"I'm comin'!" Bill shouted.

He went to grab Raffi, but the little guy was already bolting toward the noise. Bill followed, catching up easily but once again impressed by the little man's speed and gumption. It finally made sense why he first ran into the tapir all the way up at the top of the cliff, above the waterfall. He was just trying to climb as high as he could, same as Bill. It was the only way to make sense of the jungle.

The voices came loud and clear: "Bill! Up here!"

Bill's eyes followed their cries. There, in the trees, were Maia, Elena, his parents, and the rest of the Teddycats, imprisoned in what they had been led to believe would be their new den. The sight was sickening. Bill's stomach churned as he watched his friends and family press against the vines that held them in, waving their arms and howling in panic.

The closest entry point was a stand of trees to Bill's left. Under the Pets' direction, the Teddycats had built a sprawling system of shelters in the canopy, which had snapped down on them like a jaw. Bill raced up the tree and began to saw away at the vines securing the den.

"That's it, Bill!" his father encouraged. "One at a time, nice and easy."

It hurt to see Big Bill that way, helpless and horrified. Bill drove his claw into a knot of vines, but it was too thick and the rain made everything slippery. The Teddycats were bleating and shrieking in terror as an approaching presence cast a shadow on the trap. Bill turned—the sky was crowded with a swarm of Pets, claws out, preparing to attack.

A symphony of Teddycat cries: "Hurry, Bill! Save us! I don't want to die! Let me outta here!"

Bill had to stop himself from being distracted by the voices. Instead, he squeezed his eyes shut and attacked the vines with all the fury he could muster, but they shot open as an awful sound rose from the forest floor. He looked down: Raffi's body lay still in the mud, and looming over him stood Sally the Pet, licking her bloody talons.

Bill screamed with rage, and the Pets immediately set upon him, bombarding with beaks and talons. He tried to fight them off and continue slashing at the vines, but he was quickly overwhelmed. The Pets' bony wings and putrid feathers surrounded him, their weight and scent choking and oppressive. Bill snarled as he struggled to reach the top of the heap, slashing and climbing. His fury and frustration swelled until he thought he might burst. He imagined the humans ransacking Cloud Kingdom, all the friends and family Bill and the Teddycats had lost to the jungle and its ceaseless predators.

The Pets continued to pile up, nearly suffocating Bill as he lashed out with open claws, causing howls and spurts of blood.

The end felt near. The Teddycats had tried to live in the jungle—it had been a noble effort, but perhaps it was not meant to be. They had been outwitted, overpowered, late to even realize the dangers all around them. Maybe they were meant to exist only in confinement, idling among the clouds.

One voice broke through the lump of Teddycats. It was Maia. "Bill! Save yourself!"

He looked to her with pleading eyes, heart flailing. She nodded—eyes clear, jaw set and determined, Elena in her arms—and instead of helplessness Bill felt a surge of hope.

Polly and Frank flew at Bill, ready to strike, but Bill swung around the tree and, digging one claw into the trunk, lashed at his attackers with his legs. Frank careened, trying to avoid Bill's waiting claws, and smashed into a branch connected to the Teddycat trap. As Frank fell to the ground, Polly swooped down on Bill from above. Bill struck her with his claw, cutting her across the back of the wing. Off balance and out of control, she followed Frank to the forest floor, blood seeping out and staining her feathers.

The Pets continued to swarm, and Maia continued to urge Bill to abandon the Teddycats. "There's no saving us," she said. "Save yourself!"

"We love you, Bill," Marisol wailed. "Please, go! I can't watch you get ripped to shreds."

But Bill refused—this was the Teddycats' last stand. He would die fighting for their freedom.

"Not so fast!"

All the Teddycats and the Pets froze and turned toward the voice. It was Luke, leading a brigade of Olingos.

Now they were ready to rumble.

Chapter

"LUKE, YOU CAME back!" Bill hollered, heart zagging between despair and an unexpected surge of hope. Luke and the Olingos were poised in a fighting stance, their faces grim and determined.

"Luke, hold off Pablo and the Pets while Bill cuts us out of here!" shouted Maia, pressing against the vines.

"Olingos," cried Luke, "attack!"

As the Pets and the Olingos squared off on the jungle floor, Bill raced back into the trees. He embraced the mass of Teddycats through the walls of their enclosure. His mother rubbed his head in soothing circles while others yelped and begged for escape.

"Everybody quiet!" cried Maia. "We don't have much time."

The Teddycats continued to clamor and writhe.

"Hey, clamp your yaps!" snarled Diego.

"Here's the plan," said Bill. "All claws on deck: Each vine gets three Teddycats. Just keep cutting until they snap."

"They're too thick!" protested Finn the Elder.

Bill nodded. "If you can't make progress, tell me. We'll dedicate more claws until we see results. Remember, everything has a weakness—every species, every trap, every plan."

"What about the Pets?" Big Bill asked. "How long can the Olingos hold them off?"

"Our lives depend on a sketchy band of Olingos," moaned Finn. "Common jungle thieves! How has this become our fate?"

Other Teddycats joined him, sharing their concerns. "We're goners!"

"We have to trust the Olingos," said Bill. "They're our only hope of survival."

"Enough chat," said Diego. "Get to choppin'!"

Down below, the Olingos did their best to keep the Pets grounded—Pablo had two Olingos on each leg and Luke on his back, reaching for the eyes. The Pets made terrible noises as they struggled. They flashed their stolen croc teeth, chomping at the Olingos and biting down hard when they managed to catch one between their beaks.

As Bill watched the Pets fight he realized why they appeared so awkward and clumsy—they were stitched together with disparate parts, a medley of jungle species. They had all the tools but none of the savvy. The Pets had no identity, no sense of self. Their only goal was domination. The Teddycats had their claws, but without their spirit, the claws were just sharp bits of bone.

But that didn't mean the Pets weren't fierce adversaries. They were large and ruthless, and momentum was on their side.

Bill watched Sally stab at a huddled group of outmatched Olingos with her beak. Luke's cousin Roberto, an accomplished warrior and scout, pounced on her, smashing a rock against her skull, and Sally silently collapsed into a pile as the Olingos charged forward.

The Teddycats gritted their teeth as they sawed away at the vines. Finally, one popped. Bill scrambled around to the gap and pulled it as wide as it would go.

"Who can fit through this?" he yelled.

The Teddycats darted their eyes about in panic. There was no way any of their defensive experts—Big Bill, even old Diego—could wiggle between the constraints.

"I can," said a small voice. The Teddycats parted, rolling onto their sides as they sought to uncover the identity of the courageous volunteer.

It was Elena, eyes wide and brimming with fear.

Bill sized her up—she was right, she could fit. "Are you sure you can do this?"

"She's brave, and she's tested," said Maia. "She's been through this before."

It was true: Elena had survived kidnapping and imprisonment at the hands of the humans. When Bill finally found her (only after getting poached himself), she was as strong and gutsy as any of the other animals trapped in cages around her.

One by one the Teddycats stepped aside. When Elena reached the vines, she balled herself up and slithered through into Bill's waiting arms.

"Now what?" asked Elena.

Bill glanced down. The Olingos were still valiantly distracting and impeding the Pets, but it was obvious that they could only postpone the Pets' attack. Elena's claw was too short and dull to be of much use on the vines. But then Bill had an idea.

"Elena, if you follow the river all the way up to the waterfall you'll find a trail. Take it until you reach a glade, about halfway down the mountain. You'll see a trap a bit like this one, carved into the rock and filled with crocs."

The Teddycats reacted poorly to the mention of the crocs.

"What're you doing?" cried Finn.

Bill ignored them, maintaining eye contact with Elena. "Now, there might be a Pet guarding the trap. I can't be sure. If there is, try to distract them so you can unlatch the gate and let the crocs free. After that, run back to the Nest as fast as possible."

Elena didn't seem too eager to leave. She glanced longingly back at the trap and the rest of the squirming Teddycats. Bill cringed—perhaps he was asking too much. He was just about to snatch her back up when Maia cried out once more.

"Hide in the Garra den and don't go back outside until we come for you," said Maia, pleading through the vines. "I believe in you, girl: You got this."

Elena nodded, turned, and stepped into the battle.

Chapter

30

THE RAIN FELL in swoops as the sky cracked and groaned. Every few moments the canopy was splashed with bolts of light that shredded the dark clouds, only to vanish just as quickly.

Elena bopped purposefully down the tree and scurried off into the surrounding brush without attracting the Pets' attention as Bill and the other Teddycats continued to whittle and bite at the vines with their claws and teeth. They slashed and pulled, but the Pets had instructed the Teddycats to weave together hundreds of vines. Some were thick as columns.

Meanwhile, Pablo was tearing through the mob of Olingos, flinging them aside as if they were light and pesky as dragonflies. The Olingos were sopping wet and downtrodden, but they refused to back down or retreat. Time and again Luke and his father, Fred, were tossed aside, striking trees and stones as they sailed through the forest. And each time they landed with a sickening thud, then shook themselves off, regained their wits, and charged back into the fray.

Despite their panic, Bill could see the Teddycats reconsidering their long-held beliefs about the Olingos, assumptions and prejudices washing away on the rain-soaked battlefield. Their dedication and bravery would force the Teddycats—young and old—to accept them as partners and take responsibility for abandoning them for Cloud Kingdom.

At last one of the thicker vines snapped. Bill immediately gestured to his parents, but Big Bill refused. "Take Maia and Diego first," said Big Bill. "I'll be right behind with your mother."

Bill took the advice. Once Maia and Diego were on the other side of the vines, he tried to sum up what he had learned from Raffi. "The Pets want our claws. They were cursed by the humans, and now they have powers that let them take what they want from other creatures. Once they've been exposed long enough, the other species is left to die slowly."

Maia and Diego looked down on the swarm of Pets with disdain. Diego actually spit.

“I can’t believe they lied to us,” said Maia. “I feel so stupid.”

“You were brainwashed,” said Bill. “It happens to the best of us.”

“I’ll say, they aren’t looking too good, mate,” said Diego.

It was true: The Pets did appear to be in rough shape. Their feathers were no longer the same bright pink, but fading to a sickly gray as the plumage flattened beneath the weight of the rain. And their skin was further irritated, splotchy and raw. Whatever change they had hoped to trigger by defeating the Teddycats was stuck in a period of painful limbo.

“That means it’s time to strike,” said Bill.

MAIA CONTINUED TO coordinate the Teddycats’ escape while Bill and Diego raced down the tree trunk, skirting along the edge of the battle. The Olingos were slowly losing, but they had taken a lot out of the Pets. Bill believed that one final blow from their combined forces could launch the Pets out of Horizon Cove forever, and he intended to be the one to strike that blow.

As if on cue, Pablo shrieked, his beak studded with too many teeth. He flung Luke from his back and charged through the mud in the direction of Doris and Bill.

"Nobody treats my baby like that!" hollered Doris, rising up onto her hind legs.

"Uh oh," said Roberto.

"What?" said Bill.

"I take it you've never seen her like this before," said Roberto.

Doris reared up and let loose a jarring roar.

"Crikes!" said Diego, his humped back straightened in surprise.

"Yeah," said Roberto, still grimacing in pain.

"It won't be enough," said Bill. He searched the dripping wreckage of the forest for Luke or his father, but neither was back on his feet. Maia and the Teddy-cats were still clawing their way out of the tree trap. They were undermanned and outgunned. No matter how passionately Doris defended her son, Bill didn't see a way the four of them could lick Pablo on their own.

"Well, it might have to do," said Diego. He crouched into a classic Teddycat battle stance. "And if I'm goin' out, I'm goin' out with a fight."

"Me too," said Roberto, rising with a grunt.

Bill closed his eyes. There was no more time to wait for a miracle. The darkness faded as he imagined a Horizon Cove free of the Pets, their wobble and stench, lies and deceit all washed away. He saw the Teddycats and Olingos dismantling the Nest and replacing it with a strong, open community powered by trust and love as a fiery sunset between the hills lit up the valley and turned the river to silver. The Pets had taken everything the Teddycats feared about the jungle and used it against them. It was time to break free, vanquish their oppressors and their fears.

"Let's do it," said Bill.

Doris, Roberto, and Diego released whooping war cries, but Bill stayed silent as they advanced on the Pets. Pablo drove toward them, eyes and wings spread wide, a trail of feathers in his wake. The sky rumbled once more. In the scratch of light that followed, Bill was struck by an unbelievable sight.

Chapter

IN THE DISTANCE, Bill could see Elena leading the entire horde of crocs into the fray. The other Teddycats cheered from the treetops as injured Olingos rose once more to fight. The crocs were reinvigorated with freedom, snapping and biting at any Pet that crossed their path.

Elena rode on the lead croc's back like a queen.

"Meet them in the middle," hollered Bill, then he let out his first war cry and charged forward.

Pablo swung at everything in sight, but his heavy breathing betrayed his fatigue and frustration. He made eye contact with Bill and snarled. The rain poured down as they faced off on the trampled forest floor.

"It didn't have to be this way," said Bill. He could feel the rage of the crocs swelling behind him. "If you had just left before the rains . . ."

"We will never leave Horizon Cove," said Pablo. "The Teddycats are nothing. You're weaklings, never meant to live in the jungle."

Above them, Bill spotted Maia and the rest of the Teddycats. They had escaped! Silently Maia led them down from the canopy until they reached a defensive perch. Maia nodded—they were almost ready. Bill let Pablo finish his speech, buying time for the other Teddycats as they made their final preparations.

"We've run everything from hippos to humans out of here," said Pablo. "You cuddly vermin won't stop us."

Bill pounced, followed by Maia, Big Bill, and the rest of the freed Teddycats. Together they rained slashing blows down upon Pablo. Under Elena's direction, the crocs formed a protective circle, keeping other Pets from coming to the aid of their leader.

Pablo shrieked in pain as his feathers continued to fall away, exposing broken skin. The Teddycats and Olingos swarmed him until he was consumed by a writhing pile.

At last Bill called them off. The Teddycats and Olingos retreated, revealing Pablo in a bloody heap. His feathers were gone. He was plucked and beaten.

Seeing this, the crocs lunged, but Elena steered them off.

"No!" said Elena. "Don't kill them!"

Bill leaned down. Pablo's breathing was shallow and labored, but he would survive.

"How'd you do that?" Pablo muttered. "How did you gain control of the crocs and Olingos?"

"We didn't," said Bill. "We asked them for help."

The Teddycats and Olingos pushed the fallen Pets into a heap at the foot of the same grand tree that had been their prison. The Pets were bruised and battered, their signature sourness extra pungent in defeat.

Bill stood before them and narrowed his eyes. As he prepared to release his terms, he tried to channel the strength of Diego and his father, as well as the bravery and compassion of Marisol and Maia.

"Leave Horizon Cove today and never come back," said Bill, puffing his chest, "or else I'll make sure the crocs finish off every last one of you."

Chapter

THE PETS LEFT on a clear, warm morning. Though the season was far from over, the rains had momentarily ceased, and the sky was bright and fresh. Together, the Teddycats and Olingos led the birds to the edge of the clearing, with the crocs not far behind. Bill had to be honest—it would take him a while to get used to living alongside the crocs.

"Think we'll ever find Omar?" Maia asked.

"I don't know," said Bill. "That Drago was almost as creepy as Pablo. If he was still around I'm sure we would have seen him in battle."

"But what could he possibly want from Omar?" Maia wondered.

"How about this," said Bill. "Soon as the Pets leave, we send out a search party."

"Deal," said Maia.

AS THE PETS finally filed into the jungle, Big Bill, Marisol, Luke, and Diego joined Bill at Maia's side, and together the Teddycats and Olingos watched Pablo trudge into the brush.

"Well, I won't miss that fella," said Big Bill.

"Can we celebrate yet?" asked Elena, still on the back of the croc.

"There's still plenty of work to be done," said Maia. "Homes to rebuild, wounds to heal."

"The last party we had was interrupted by the crocs," said Bill.

"But now they're our friends!" said Elena.

"That's reason enough to party right there," said Diego. "Pals with a croc. Never thought I'd see the day."

"We almost didn't," said Marisol. "Luke, have the Olingos decided where you want to build your den?"

"We're itchin' to mark the occasion, too!" said Luke. "So long, dirty birds!"

The Teddycats and Olingos waved as the Pets disappeared into the wilderness. Horizon Cove felt huge and welcoming, stuffed with food, drink, and shelter. Bill's heart felt equally full, brimming with love and relief. The journey that began with banishment from Cloud Kingdom was finally over, and they were closer than ever to becoming true citizens of the jungle.

Teddycats and Olingos began to make their way through the clearing and down to the garden. They found warm rocks on which to sun themselves and called out for the others to join them.

Bill found his family and settled in the sunshine. When Finn and Armado first approached, Big Bill scowled in their direction. But Bill beckoned them closer.

"You bravely defended our civilization, Bill Garra," said Finn. The two Elders had their heads down, hanging against their gray scruff. "We know now that the only way to survive is to keep moving forward."

"We just want to help," Armando croaked.

Marisol gave Bill's shoulders a loving squeeze with the same healing paws that had brought Felix and so many other innocent animals to Cloud Kingdom for care and protection. He knew then that Horizon Cove would be a refuge for all who sought peace.

Bill hopped off the warm stone and landed on a patch of the Pets' pink flowers. He pulled up a bunch with his claws and smiled at the Elders.

"Don't worry," said Bill. "There's still plenty of work to be done."

THE END